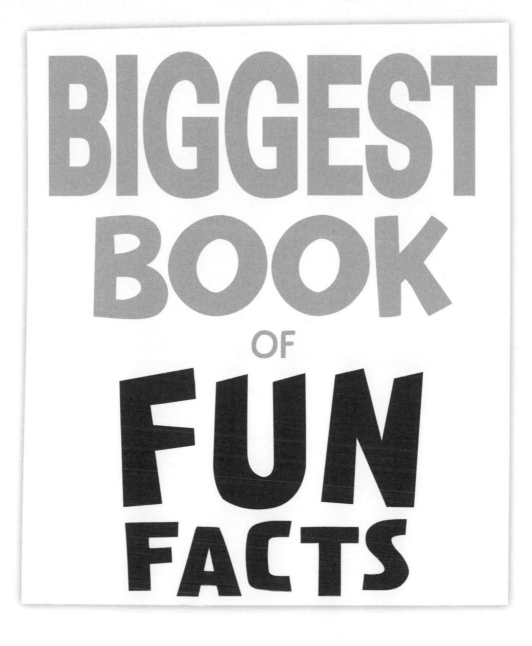

BIGGEST BOOK OF FUN FACTS

Text by
Amanda Ericson, Gail Herman, Sarah Kincius, Esther Reisberg, Isabella Simon

Photo Credits
Dreamstime, iClipart, iStockphoto

Kidsbooks®

Copyright © 2019 Kidsbooks, LLC
3535 West Peterson Avenue
Chicago, IL 60659

Every effort has been made to ensure all information and photographs in this book are correct.

032002032GD
Printed in China

***Visit us at* www.kidsbookspublishing.com**

Get ready to learn about our wonderful world through fascinating and
FUN FACTS!

Find out:

- Which inventions were created by accident
- What is the stinkiest fruit on the planet
- Which favorite animated movie hero was originally a villain
- Where you can find the world's wackiest landmarks
- Which First Lady was a professional dancer
- Fantastic facts about record breakers, mythical monsters, historic moments, and the arts

And much, much more!

Also includes Search & Find® puzzles, word searches, mazes, and other fun activities!

Get ready to impress your family and friends with your newfound knowledge!

Kidsbooks®

And Now, for the Weather

The average hurricane releases an incredible amount of energy: 200 times the largest amount of electricity that the world's generators are capable of producing!

Running Hot and Cold

In Oklahoma City, on November 11, 1911, the temperature dropped from 83°F to 17°F. That's a 66-degree difference in one day!

HEAT WAVE

The hottest air temperature ever recorded was in Death Valley, California, in the United States. On July 10, 1913, Death Valley was recorded to be 134° Fahrenheit (F)! The ground is even hotter there: In 1972, the ground temperature was 201°F!

134°

Should I Wear a Jacket?

Crickets change their chirps according to the weather, and there's a formula to figure out the temperature based on this: Count the number of chirps you hear in 15 seconds, then add 37.

Up and Down

On January 22, 1943, Spearfish, South Dakota, broke the record for biggest temperature change in two minutes. The thermometer rose from -4°F to 45°F, thanks to a long, dry wind that swept through town.

Rainy Day Colors

During the summer of 2001, red rain—the color of blood—repeatedly fell on the southwestern state of Kerala, India. Some people reported seeing green, black, and yellow raindrops!

FREEZE YOU OUT

The coldest place on Earth is Antarctica! In winter, the sun never rises, and the temperature on the East Antarctic Plateau has been recorded at -144°F—so cold that no human could breathe in without damaging his or her lungs.

Making It Rain

The city on Earth with the most rainfall is Mawsynram, India. During monsoon season, from May to October, almost 36 feet of rain falls each year!

A Mighty Wind

The strongest wind ever recorded happened in Oklahoma during a tornado in 1999, which reached 302 miles per hour (mph)!

THE DRIEST PLACE ON EARTH IS IN A PLACE CALLED THE DRY VALLEYS IN ANTARCTICA, WHICH HAS HAD NO RAIN OR SNOW FOR NEARLY 2 MILLION YEARS!

No Business Like Show Business

Broadway, in New York City's theater district, has 40 different theaters showing plays and musicals every night.

Broadway is known as the Great White Way because of all the bright electric lights from the billboards advertising shows.

The character of Elphaba in the Broadway smash *Wicked* got her name from the initials of *The Wizard of Oz* author L. Frank Baum.

About TWO-THIRDS of Broadway audience members are FEMALE.

Off and Off-Off

A Broadway show gets its name from its size: New York's Broadway theaters seat 500 people each, off-Broadway shows hold 100 to 499, and off-off-Broadway theaters have fewer than 100 seats.

SHAKESPEARE'S CURSE

Broadway actors know that it's bad luck to say the word "MacBeth" out loud in a theater—even if they're acting in the Shakespeare play! Instead, people call *MacBeth* "the Scottish Play."

"PHAN" FAVORITE

The longest-running musical on Broadway is *The Phantom of the Opera*. It has been performed more than 12,000 times since it opened in 1988!

Crossword Puzzle

All the World's a Stage

Complete the crossword using the clues below.

ACROSS

5. To try out for a part
6. A play with song and dance routines
8. The break between acts
9. You need this to see a show at the theater

DOWN

1. Furniture, pictures, or anything used onstage to create a setting
2. A serious play, without music
3. Musicians play in the _____
4. It's called the Great White Way because of all the bright _____
5. People who watch the show
7. All the actors in a play

Answers on page 298

Just Desserts

Make sure to observe National Dessert Day— October 14.

How the Cookie Crumbled

The chocolate chip cookie was invented by Ruth Wakefield by accident in 1937. Wakefield was trying to make a chocolate cookie, but the chocolate pieces in the dough didn't blend in, and she ended up with chocolate chip cookies instead.

You don't order dessert in England; you order "pudding."

THE WORD "DESSERT" COMES FROM THE FRENCH WORD *DESSERVIR*, ORIGINALLY MEANING "TO REMOVE WHAT HAS BEEN SERVED"— IN THIS CASE, DISHES FROM THE MAIN COURSE.

Marshmallows were originally made from the root of the marsh mallow plant, used to treat sore throats and stomach problems.

The Stinky Twinkie

The world's oldest Twinkie can be found at a high school in Maine. Unwrapped in 1976 as part of a science experiment on preservatives, it now sits in a glass case in the dean's office—uneaten and still in one piece.

Cash or Cupcake?

In some US cities, residents can go to their local Sprinkles bakery and use an ATM to get cupcakes instead of money.

THE MOST-GOOGLED RECIPE IN 2018 WAS PECAN PIE.

Fudge is thought to have been created in the late 1880s when an American baker trying to make caramels made a mistake and said,

"OH, FUDGE!"

The **Tour de Donut** is a 32-mile bike race held in various **US** cities, in which **participants** get to shave **five minutes** off their finish times for every **donut** they **eat** throughout the **ride**.

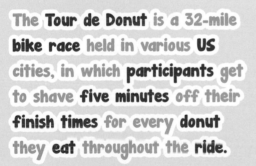

A Recipe Record

The world's biggest gingerbread house, created in 2013 in Bryan, Texas, included 1,800 pounds of butter, 7,200 eggs, and 3½ tons of flour, among other ingredients. Standing 21 feet high, the house was almost as big as a tennis court, with more than 22,000 pieces of candy decorations.

IN THE PAST, JELL-O FLAVORS HAVE INCLUDED CELERY, TOMATO, COLA, AND MAPLE SYRUP.

Hooray for PB&J!

THE FIRST RECIPE FOR A PEANUT BUTTER AND JELLY (PB&J) SANDWICH APPEARED IN THE *BOSTON COOKING SCHOOL MAGAZINE OF CULINARY SCIENCE AND DOMESTIC ECONOMICS,* BY JULIA DAVID CHANDLER, IN 1901.

The average American will eat about 1,500 PB&J sandwiches by the time he or she is 18 years old, and 3,000 in a lifetime.

Even people who are allergic to peanuts and nuts can enjoy a delicious PB&J sandwich by using a surprising peanut butter substitute—Sunflower seed butter!

The world's
BIGGEST
PB&J sandwich was made November 13, 2010, at the Great American Peanut Butter Festival in Grand Saline, Texas, and weighed
1,342 POUNDS.

MAKING THE CUT

The PB&J sandwich became a lunch box regular with the help of a 1928 invention—sliced bread. A jeweler named Otto Rohwedder built the first slicing machine.

THE ORIGINS OF PEANUT BUTTER GO BACK 3,000 YEARS TO THE ANCIENT AZTECS AND INCAS—THE FIRST PEOPLE TO TURN PEANUTS INTO PASTE.

SPACE LUNCH

Astronauts at the International Space Station use tortillas to make their PB&J sandwiches. They also use tape and Velcro, so the ingredients won't float away!

Nutty but True

Though he was a world-renowned inventor, George Washington Carver did not invent peanut butter. He did discover 300 other uses for peanuts, including making soap, glue, and paper.

THE PEANUT IS NOT A NUT. IT IS A LEGUME, LIKE PEAS AND BEANS.

IT'S A MOUTHFUL

Can you say the word

"ARACHIBUTYROPHOBIA"?

It is the fear of peanut butter sticking to the roof of your mouth.

The first known cookbook, written in the 1st century AD, included a recipe for jam.

Doctor's Orders

A food company's use of Dr. Ambrose Straub's patented peanut butter machine at the 1904 St. Louis World's Fair brought peanut butter to the general public. Soon, grocery stores began ordering it— and the rest is peanut butter history.

Fine Dining

In the early 1900s, peanut butter was served at fancy New York City tearooms and elegant parties. It was considered a gourmet treat!

Rover to the Rescue

MEDICINE RUN

Balto may be the most famous dog of all time. In 1925, the Siberian husky led his dogsled team through a blinding blizzard, traveling over 55 miles in 20 hours to bring emergency medicine to the children of Nome, Alaska. The annual Iditarod Trail Sled Dog Race is held in his honor.

LONG WAY DOWN

On September 11, 2001, there were terrorist attacks on the World Trade Center in New York City. Guide dog Roselle led her owner Michael Hingson, who is blind, to safety down 78 floors, helping those around her stay calm, too.

FIERY ESCAPE

In 1991, Kathe Vaughn, paralyzed from the waist down, panicked when her van caught on fire and she couldn't escape. It's a good thing Eve was traveling along: The six-year-old Rottweiler grabbed her leg and pulled her out before the van exploded.

Doggy Clean-Up

Paris, a boxer in Cornwall, England, made news in 2016 for helping to save the planet. How? By picking up cans and plastic bottles during walks, then dropping them in recycling bins.

POOCH PATROL.

In 2008, Treo, a black Labrador retriever who served with the British military, sniffed out bombs in war-torn Afghanistan on at least two separate occasions, saving countless lives. He retired a decorated war hero.

Prize-Winning Save

In 2011, the Dog of the Year Award was given to a golden retriever named Yogi. When Yogi's owner Paul Horton flipped off his bicycle far from home and couldn't move, Yogi ran for help, bringing neighbors back to assist Paul.

All Choked Up

Debbie Parkhurst was at her Maryland home with her dog, Toby, in 2007, when Parkhurst choked on an apple. Toby pushed her to the floor to perform a doggy version of the Heimlich maneuver—and this time, it worked!

To the Rescue

In 2007, a Doberman pinscher named Khan spied a deadly snake in his family's backyard and leapt into action to save 17-month-old Charlotte, picking her up by the diaper to move her away.

Call for Help

A trained service dog named Yolanda called 911 from a special phone and saved her owner's life—twice! In 2014, she called for help when Maria Colon, who is blind, fell and lost consciousness. In 2015, she called again when their Philadelphia home was on fire.

That Sinking Feeling

Watch Out!

If you step in quicksand, you can sink. Quicksand is just regular sand, but it's so waterlogged and loose, it can't hold any weight.

Don't Panic!

In reality, it is difficult to drown in quicksand. You won't sink past your legs. Experts say to stay calm and move slowly back and forth to loosen the sand's hold.

WHEN ELSE DOES THE GROUND GIVE WAY? WITH A SINKHOLE, THE GROUND SUDDENLY COLLAPSES, LEAVING A HOLE THAT SWALLOWS ANYTHING ON THE SURFACE.

HORSING AROUND

In 2017, a horse got stuck in quicksand on a beach in Belgium, and the tide was coming in fast. While a truck dumped sand to block the rising water, firefighters and beachgoers dug him out by hand.

Starring: Quicksand

Quicksand was a common feature in old adventure movies. A jungle explorer would unwittingly step in a sand pit, then sink lower... lower...lower...until he or she would disappear.

Presidential Pit

In May 2018, a sinkhole suddenly appeared on the White House lawn. There was no danger; it was only about 8 inches wide.

GOING BATTY

THE DEVIL'S SINKHOLE IN ROCK SPRINGS, TEXAS, IS A NATIONAL NATURAL LANDMARK AND A GIANT HOME FOR BATS: THREE MILLION HAVE BEEN SPOTTED FLYING OUT OF THE 140-FOOT-DEEP HOLE.

Clothes Call

In Guatemala City, an entire clothing factory disappeared inside a 100-foot-deep, perfectly round sinkhole in June 2010. The factory was empty, so no one was hurt.

A 40-foot-wide sinkhole in Bowling Green, Kentucky's National Corvette Museum swallowed eight classic cars in 2012 and caused millions of dollars in damage.

MEGA SINKHOLE!

The world's deepest sinkhole is the Xiaozhal Tiankeng in China. It measures 2,040 feet—about one-and-a-half Empire State Buildings can fit inside.

Florida has had more sinkholes than any other state. A region in Central Florida is even called Sinkhole Alley.

Welcome to
FLORIDA
THE SINKHOLE STATE

What in the Worlds?

In 5 billion years, scientists predict the sun will become a red giant, a dying star that will cool down and change shade and shape.

CHECK THE THERMOMETER!

Mercury has daytime temperatures of around 800°F, but at night they can drop close to -300°F. That's more than a 1,000-degree difference in one day!

EARTH is the ONLY planet NOT named after a GREEK or ROMAN god.

Sun

Mercury

Venus

Earth

Mars

The days on Venus are so long that just one is equal to 243 days on Earth!

More than 100 Martian rocks have been discovered on Earth—some in Antarctica and the Sahara Desert!

There is a giant system of canyons on Mars called Valles Marineris that is as long as the United States.

Mars has the biggest volcano that we know of in the solar system.

A STRANGE SPIN

Venus and Uranus spin the wrong way—or at least a different way! The two planets turn in the opposite direction of the other planets.

Earth rotation

Venus rotation

SATURN AND JUPITER EACH HAVE MORE THAN 60 MOONS.

Uranus and Neptune are called ice giants because they're the coldest planets, located farthest from the sun.

Jupiter

Saturn

Uranus

Neptune

?

JUPITER IS SO BIG THAT IT CAN FIT OVER 1,000 EARTHS INSIDE!

Planet Downgrade

It's possible for a planet to lose its planetary status! Pluto was officially a planet until 2006, when scientists decided it was actually a dwarf planet, not a real one.

In 2015, NASA's *New Horizons* spacecraft took pictures that showed an astounding discovery—1000-foot icy mountains exist on Pluto.

WEIGHING IN

If you weigh 100 pounds on Earth, you would weigh 38 pounds on Mercury and 234 pounds on Jupiter. The smaller the planet, the weaker the gravity, the less you weigh!

How Did They Think of That?

Engineer Richard James was working on a new kind of spring for navigation instruments when he accidentally knocked some springs off a shelf. The springs "stepped" across the floor, and— voilà—he had the toy we now know as the

SLINKY!

© Edgars Sermulis | Dreamstime.com

Cleaner or Clay?

While working for a soap company, the McVicker family created a soft, squishy material to clean walls. One family member—a teacher—realized it could work as modeling clay and brought it to her classroom, and it became Play-Doh!

A REVOLUTIONARY IDEA

Thomas Jefferson liked to move around while he worked. In 1775, he came up with a desk chair that moved, too: the first swivel chair. It is believed he sat in that very chair while writing the Declaration of Independence!

MELTED MESS

Percy Spencer, an engineer working with energy waves called microwaves on radar systems, stood in front of one device and realized it had melted the candy bar in his pocket. Can you guess the kitchen appliance Spencer invented in 1945?

Inspiration Calls

In 1973, Martin Cooper—inspired by high-tech communicators from the *Star Trek* TV series—created the first cell phone. It took about a decade for the big, bulky phone to go on sale.

Dish Glitch

Wealthy Josephine Cochcrane was so annoyed by her household staff chipping plates while they washed dishes that she decided to do them herself. When that grew tiring, she invented the first automatic dishwasher, receiving a patent in 1886.

A Sticky Solution

While walking in the woods, Swiss engineer Georges de Mestral became intrigued with the burrs that stuck to his dog's fur. He recreated the effect with Velcro, a combination of the words "velvet" and "crochet."

Stuff Your Poker Face

Legend has it that in the late 1700s, England's Earl of Sandwich couldn't bear to leave the card table while playing poker. He requested a piece of meat stuffed between two slices of toast so he could eat with one hand and play cards with the other—and his "sandwich" caught on.

All Clear!

Mary Anderson rode a New York City trolley car in 1902 and watched the driver lean outside to wipe falling snow from the windshield. Back home in Alabama—where it hardly ever snowed, and she never even drove—Anderson came up with a window-cleaning device for vehicles:

WINDSHIELD WIPERS!

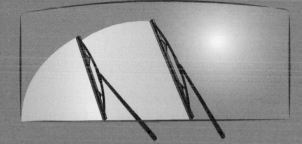

Every Body Is Amazing

Hold your arms out straight and measure the distance across:

5'6"

That's your height!

What's Up, Bud?

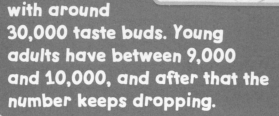

Babies are born with around 30,000 taste buds. Young adults have between 9,000 and 10,000, and after that the number keeps dropping.

TWENTY-FIVE PERCENT OF ADULT BONES ARE IN THE FEET.

YOU PRODUCE MORE EARWAX WHEN YOU'RE FRIGHTENED.

 People spend about five years of their lives eating and a whopping 26 years sleeping!

The space between your eyebrows is called the glabella.

The Write Nails

Fingernails grow fastest on your writing hand and your longest fingers!

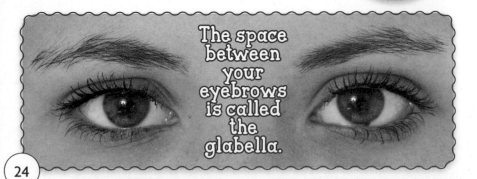

Crack the Code

The Human Body

Use the key below to find out the
answers to these human body riddles.

1=H	5=G	9=Q	13=Z	17=S	21=L	25=C
2=M	6=O	10=D	14=F	18=Y	22=V	26=K
3=E	7=A	11=W	15=J	19=B	23=I	
4=P	8=T	12=N	16=U	20=X	24=R	

What are 10 things you can always count on?

$\overline{18}$ $\overline{6}$ $\overline{16}$ $\overline{24}$　$\overline{14}$ $\overline{23}$ $\overline{12}$ $\overline{5}$ $\overline{3}$ $\overline{24}$ $\overline{17}$

What is the most musical bone?

　　　　　　　　-

$\overline{8}$ $\overline{1}$ $\overline{3}$　$\overline{8}$ $\overline{24}$ $\overline{6}$ $\overline{2}$　$\overline{19}$ $\overline{6}$ $\overline{12}$ $\overline{3}$

Why is your nose in the middle of your face?

$\overline{19}$ $\overline{3}$ $\overline{25}$ $\overline{7}$ $\overline{16}$ $\overline{17}$ $\overline{3}$　$\overline{23}$ $\overline{8}$　$\overline{23}$ $\overline{17}$

$\overline{8}$ $\overline{1}$ $\overline{3}$　$\overline{17}$ $\overline{25}$ $\overline{3}$ $\overline{12}$ $\overline{8}$ $\overline{3}$ $\overline{24}$

What did the left hand say to the other hand when they argued?

$\overline{11}$ $\overline{1}$ $\overline{18}$　$\overline{7}$ $\overline{24}$ $\overline{3}$　$\overline{18}$ $\overline{6}$ $\overline{16}$

$\overline{7}$ $\overline{21}$ $\overline{11}$ $\overline{7}$ $\overline{18}$ $\overline{17}$　$\overline{24}$ $\overline{23}$ $\overline{5}$ $\overline{1}$ $\overline{8}$?

Answers on page 299

Eat Your Fruits and Veggies

What's What?
Think string beans, cucumbers, and peppers are vegetables? Think again. Scientifically, they're fruit! Fruits have seeds, and veggies don't.

Each pomegranate has between **600** and **1,000** seeds.

Making a Stink
The durian, grown in Southeast Asia, is considered the world's stinkiest fruit. People have compared it to smelly gym socks, and it has been banned from Singapore trains and buses.

Follow the Bouncing Berry
Ripe cranberries bounce like balls. Growers say the bigger the bounce, the better the berry!

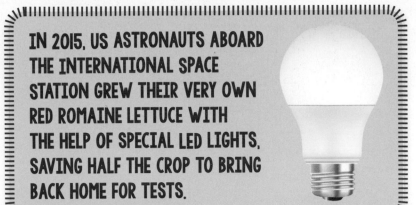

IN 2015, US ASTRONAUTS ABOARD THE INTERNATIONAL SPACE STATION GREW THEIR VERY OWN RED ROMAINE LETTUCE WITH THE HELP OF SPECIAL LED LIGHTS, SAVING HALF THE CROP TO BRING BACK HOME FOR TESTS.

Oranges grown in hot, sunny places near the equator stay green even when ripe, but they're dyed or treated so customers can get the orange color they expect.

BERRY TRUE

True berries have seeds inside, like cranberries and blueberries. By that definition, strawberries aren't berries, and bananas are!

The Ripe Choice

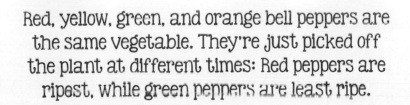

Red, yellow, green, and orange bell peppers are the same vegetable. They're just picked off the plant at different times: Red peppers are ripest, while green peppers are least ripe.

Pack It for School

Don't forget to put a cucumber in your pencil case. It can be used as an eraser!

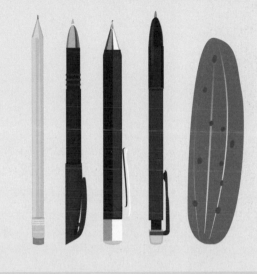

A Higher Ruling

FRUIT

VEGGIE

Even though the tomato is scientifically a fruit, in 1893 the Supreme Court ruled it was a vegetable because most people viewed it that way.

27

It's Friday the 13th!

January

Sunday	Monday	Tuesday	Wednesday	Thursday	Friday	Saturday
1	2	3	4	5	6	7
8	9	10	11	12	(13)	14
		17	18	19	20	21
		24	25			28
29	30	31				

UNLUCKY 17
THIRTEEN is considered a LUCKY number in ITALY. Their UNLUCKY day is Friday the 17TH.

Every year has at least one Friday the 13th, but, luckily, there can't be more than three.

In the 1930s and '40s, the people of French Lick, Indiana, decided that every black cat must wear a bell around its neck on Friday the 13th so people could avoid it.

The unlucky day inspired a scary movie series and a TV show called— what else?— Friday the 13th.

OVER A FOUR-DAY PERIOD IN 2012, DOZENS OF TORNADOES STRUCK OKLAHOMA— AND IT ALL BEGAN ON APRIL 13, A FRIDAY.

Some sources report airfares are lower on Friday the 13th to encourage superstitious flyers to buy tickets.

Not Quite a Holiday

Each year, Finland marks one Friday the 13th to observe National Accident Day. The goal: to raise safety awareness on a day when people are expecting more accidents.

Mr. Rogers, beloved creator and star of *Mister Rogers' Neighborhood*, named one of his puppets King Friday XIII, so children would think the day was fun, not unlucky.

It was bad luck for the passengers aboard the *Costa Concordia* when the cruise ship began to sink off the Italian coast on Friday, January 13, 2012.

Happy Birthday, Taylor

IN DECEMBER 2002, TAYLOR SWIFT TURNED 13 ON FRIDAY THE 13TH, BUT THAT WAS OKAY WITH HER. IT'S HER FAVORITE NUMBER!

In some Spanish-speaking countries, people are superstitious about **Tuesday** the 13th.

Tuesday
13
February

Twins, Triplets, and More

BY THE NUMBERS

There are at least 125 million "multiples" around the world. These include twins (2), triplets (3), quadruplets (4), quintuplets (5), sextuplets (6), septuplets (7), octuplets (8), and nonuplets (9).

One in a Million

The odds of twin sisters delivering twin babies on the same day are about 1 in a million, but Andrea Springer and Ashlee Means had their twin boys on the same day—December 14, 2004.

Parents can have "mixed" triplets— two identical children and one fraternal.

Twin Jims

Identical twin boys adopted into different families didn't know each other existed until they met at age 39. Amazingly, they were both named Jim, owned dogs named Toy, bit their nails, worked as sheriffs, married women named Linda, then divorced and married women named Betty!

Identical twins don't have identical **fingerprints.**

TWINS are TWICE as LIKELY to be LEFT-HANDED as the REST of the POPULATION.

MANY SETS OF TWINS DEVELOP THEIR OWN LANGUAGES.

Multiple Multiples

The *Guinness Book of World Records* cites Valentina Vassilyev, an 18th century Russian peasant, for giving birth to 69 children: four sets of quadruplets, seven sets of triplets, and 16 pairs of twins!

Mirror, Mirror on the Wall

About 25% of all twins are mirror images, exact reflections of one another. If one is right-handed, the other is left-handed, and so on.

TALL women are more likely to have twins.

Trending Now

IF YOU HAVE ONE SOCIAL MEDIA ACCOUNT, CHANCES ARE YOU HAVE SIX MORE: THE AVERAGE USER HAS 7.6 ACCOUNTS.

The first Instagram post ever was a photo taken by cofounder Kevin Systrom of a stray dog sitting near a taco stand in Mexico.

After just two months, Instagram had **1 MILLION USERS.**

Twitter's little blue bird is named Larry, for basketball legend Larry Bird of the Boston Celtics.

More than 300 hours of video is uploaded to YouTube every minute.

You Tube

WHAT'S THE MOST POPULAR FOOD PICTURED ON INSTAGRAM?

PIZZA!

Twitter's most popular emoji is the happy face, crying tears of joy.

In 2018, **Katy Perry** had the most Twitter followers, with **Justin Bieber** coming in second, and **Barack Obama** third— each with over

100 million!

The average Twitter user has 707 followers, but 391 million accounts have no followers at all.

All together, people on Snapchat view about 8 billion videos per day.

After one day in operation, Facebook had **1,200** members.

Snapchat was originally called Picaboo, but the name was already being used.

Searching for Meaning

Google

Google Search   I'm Feeling Lucky

Google gets about 40,000 searches every second.

INDIA has more Facebook users than any other country.

All Aboard the Mayflower

On August 5, 1620, the *Mayflower* set sail from England to America with a boatload of passengers—though it wasn't a passenger ship at all. It was built for transporting products around Europe, not for long voyages! With high winds and storms, the 3,000-mile trip took twice as long as expected.

Odor Alert

It was a messy, stinky voyage. No one could wash clothes, bathe, or shower.

THERE WERE MORE THAN TWICE AS MANY MALE PASSENGERS AS FEMALE, AND ABOUT A THIRD OF THE GROUP WERE CHILDREN.

FOUR-LEGGED PASSENGERS

The *Mayflower* carried at least two dogs, a mastiff and an English springer spaniel. Most likely, passengers brought pigs, goats, chickens, and cats, while rats probably came with the ship!

34

SOME PASSENGERS HAD UNUSUAL NAMES, SUCH AS LOVE, WRESTLING, RESOLVED, AND REMEMBER!

The ship carried about **12 cannons**, in case of pirate attacks.

About 35 MILLION Americans are descended from *Mayflower* passengers.

ONE PASSENGER DIED DURING THE JOURNEY, A SERVANT NAMED WILLIAM BUTTEN, JUST DAYS BEFORE SIGHTING LAND.

A barn in Jordana, England, is said to have been built with planks from the *Mayflower*, retrieved when the ship was sold for scrap in 1624.

One baby was born during the journey, a boy fittingly named Oceanus.

Shore to Shore

Want to feel like a Pilgrim? Visit the *Mayflower II*, a recreation of the original ship. It sailed from Plymouth, England, to Plymouth, Massachusetts, in 1957, where it docked close to Plimoth Plantation and became a floating museum.

Take Me Out
to the Ballgame

Senior Stadium

Fenway Park is the oldest baseball park still in use. The home of the Boston Red Sox opened on April 20, 1912.

BLINK AND YOU'D MISS IT

The shortest game ever played was only 51 minutes long, on September 28, 1919, when the New York Giants defeated the Philadelphia Phillies, 6-1.

Perfect Attendance

Oriole shortstop Cal Ripken Jr. didn't miss a single game from April 30, 1982, to September 19, 1998. He played for 16 years in 2,632 straight games!

Each baseball is hand-stitched with exactly 108 stitches.

IN THE DARK

Wrigley Field (pictured here), home of the Chicago Cubs, opened in 1914 but didn't hold a night game until 1988. Why? It was the very last stadium to put in lights.

The Long Game

The longest game on record was played in 1984 over two days. The matchup between the Chicago White Sox and the Milwaukee Brewers lasted eight hours and six minutes, with 25 innings and a 7-6 Sox win.

Approximately 600,000 baseballs are used by the major leagues during one season—70 balls for each game.

Batter Up!

In 1929, the Yankees were the first team to put numbers on the backs of uniforms. The numbers were based on batting order, so Babe Ruth and Lou Gehrig wore numbers "3" and "4."

What a Team!

Ken Griffey Sr. and Ken Griffey Jr. became the first father and son to play for the same team when Griffey Jr. joined the Seattle Mariners in 1990. On September 14 of that same year, they hit back-to-back home runs!

Zany Name, USA

BORING, OREGON, isn't boring; it just took the name of its first settler, William Harrison Boring.

A Sure Sign
How did NO NAME, COLORADO, get its name? One story tells that a highway worker realized the region had never been named, so he wrote "No Name" on a sign by Exit 119—and it stuck.

WHEN IT WAS FOUNDED IN 1977, FOUR PEOPLE LIVED IN NOTHING, ARIZONA.

Why "Why"?
At one time, two state roads near the Mexican border formed a "Y" shape near a community. Since Arizona law stated that the names of all cities and towns must have at least three letters, the town became WHY, ARIZONA!

EXIT 119
NO NAME ↗

NOTHING

A Fowl Name
During the Gold Rush, a group of prospectors survived an Alaska winter by hunting the ptarmigan and wanted to name their town after the bird—but no one knew how to spell it. They settled for CHICKEN, ALASKA.

IT'S THE TRUTH
In 1950, a town called Hot Springs changed its name to the title of a radio game show called *Truth or Consequences*. Every year, TRUTH OR CONSEQUENCES, NEW MEXICO, hosts the Truth or Consequences Fiesta.

How Embarrassing!

When French explorers had trouble canoeing down a Minnesota river, they called the area Embarras, for the French word meaning "to hinder, confuse, or complicate." We now know the city as EMBARRASS, MINNESOTA.

A Very Merry Town

In 1856, townspeople in Santa Fe, INDIANA, realized there was another Santa Fe close by. They wanted to keep "Santa" and change the rest, but the only name they could come up with was SANTA CLAUS!

This Land Is Your Land, This Land Is My Land

As legend has it, two men surveying land claimed the exact same site by accident. The name stuck: ACCIDENT, MARYLAND.

FRANKENSTEIN, MISSOURI's name has nothing to do with the monster; it's named for Gottfried Franken, who gave the town his land in the late 1800s.

Why Not?

WHYNOT, NORTH CAROLINA: Town settlers couldn't decide on a name until one man suggested, "Why not call the town, 'Whynot'?" and everyone agreed.

Name of Town **Uncertain**

When residents of one unnamed town in TEXAS had to fill out a questionnaire, many wrote UNCERTAIN on the line marked "Name of Town," and you can guess what happened!

EXPERIMENT, GEORGIA, was named for an agricultural research station at nearby University of Georgia, the Georgia Experiment Station.

Into the Wild

FEET FIRMLY PLANTED

Elephants, like hippos and rhinos, are too big to jump. However, the elephant is the only four-legged animal that can't lift all its legs at the same time when it runs.

DROPPING BY

Bats hang upside down while they sleep so they can drop from their perches, spread their wings, and quickly fly away. With teeny, tiny legs, they would have a much harder time taking off from the ground.

A koala bear's fingerprints are so similar to a human's, its prints confuse scientists!

True Stripes

Zebras are black with white stripes—not the other way around. The white stripes appear because of an absence of pigment.

Lions need a lot of sleep—between 16 and 20 hours a day!

THE ANTEATER HAS THE **LONGEST** TONGUE OF ANY ANIMAL.

SKIN DEEP

A tiger's skin has stripes in the exact same pattern as its fur.

NO GOING BACK

Kangaroos can hop to it, but they can't hop—or even walk—backward. Their tails would get in the way.

A BONY QUESTION

Giraffes have seven bones in their necks—the same number of bones as humans and almost every other mammal, even mice! How is that possible? It's all a matter of size: Giraffe bones are almost a foot long.

Hippos can't swim; they just wade through water!

PRAIRIE DOGS KISS WHEN THEY MEET—BUT IF THEY'RE NOT IN THE SAME GROUP, A FIGHT COULD BREAK OUT AFTER THE SMOOCH!

Celebration!

Short Work of It

Bermuda Day is observed each May in—where else?—Bermuda! It celebrates the island's heritage and marks the start of summer—and the first day of the year when it's officially okay to wear shorts to work.

NIGHT OF THE RADISHES

This Mexican holiday, celebrated in Oaxaca, is a festival of the vegetable. It's held every December 23, with radishes carved into figures and scenes, including Christmas-themed displays.

Twice as Nice

The Korean alphabet is so important, its creation—back in the 15th century—is celebrated twice: during South Korea's Hangul Day on October 9, and North Korea's Chosongul Day January 1.

A Time for Reflection

Nyepi Day is observed on the island of Bali, on the night of a new moon in early spring. Considered a kind of new year, people spend the day at home, deep in thought—no talking, watching TV, or using electricity allowed. The streets are empty, except for police patrolling to make sure everyone stays inside.

Thanksgiving in the Jungle

Monkeys love the Monkey Banquet Festival in Lopburi, Thailand, a village near the jungle. On the last weekend of November, long tables of food (lots of veggies, fruit, and rice) are set up by an old ruin, and thousands of wild monkeys attend, bringing luck to the villagers.

It's a G'Day, Mate!

BOTTLER!

BONZA!

Since August 8, 1985, Australians have marked Bonza Bottler Day once a month, when the number of the month matches the date.

In Australia, *bonza* is slang for "great," and *bottler* is slang for "something excellent."

Take the Leap!

Leap Day comes once every four years, along with Sadie Hawkins Day. Originating from a 1937 comic strip called Li'l Abner and a character named Sadie Hawkins, it's the day women, who traditionally had to be invited by men to go to a dance, have the chance to ask out who they want to take to the Sadie Hawkins Dance.

TOMATINA

It's a holiday and a giant food fight rolled into one, when thousands of visitors flock to Buñol, Spain, to throw tomatoes. Trucks deliver loads of tomatoes up and down the streets, and people make their reservations early—tickets are always sold out.

British Royalty Rules

Watch the Queen Carefully

When the queen stops eating, everyone else must stop. When she stands, everyone stands as well.

A "No" Vote

The royal family does not vote. They are not supposed to take sides in politics.

VOTE

A Rule for the Birds

Six ravens must always be kept at the Tower of London. Why? An old legend states that if the ravens leave the tower, the kingdom will fall.

Married women in the royal family must wear hats to official events and swap those hats for tiaras after 6:00 P.M.

Royal family members are not allowed to take selfies.

She Gets a Pass

The queen can drive, even without a license. She doesn't need a passport either.

NO DICE

No one in the royal family is allowed to play Monopoly. The game is considered too competitive.

Napkin Nicety

If you're eating dinner with the royal family, fold your napkin in half after each use. It's the proper (and expected) thing to do.

Royal Maze

Have Crown, Will Travel

Follow the maze from start to finish to help the queen go from Buckingham Palace in London to her country estate Windsor Castle.

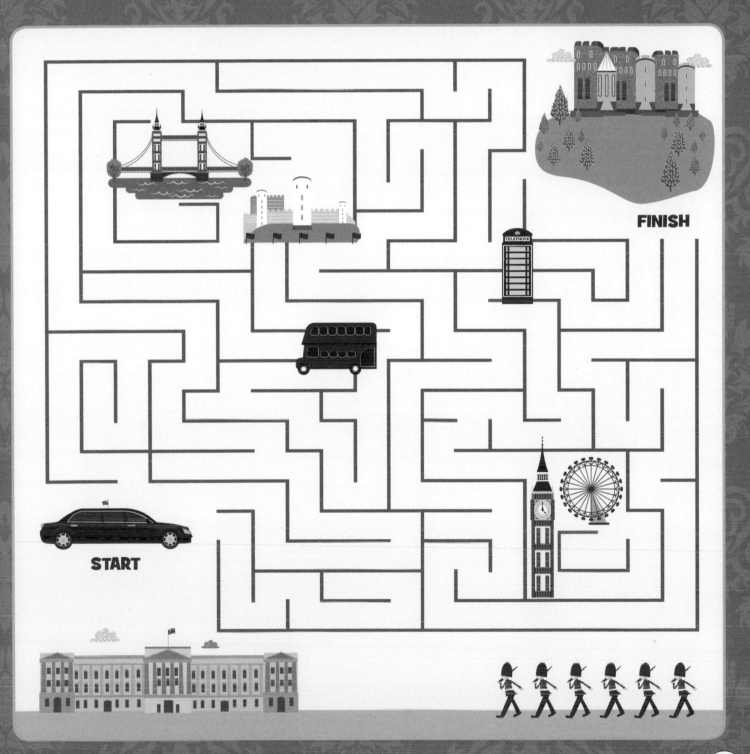

FINISH

START

Top of the World
The North Pole

The North Pole is the northernmost spot on Earth, where there's nowhere else to go but down (south).

ELLESMERE ISLAND IN CANADA'S NUNAVUT TERRITORY IS THE CLOSEST PIECE OF LAND TO THE NORTH POLE, 447 MILES AWAY.

THERE IS NO LAND AT ALL AT THE NORTH POLE— JUST SNOW, ICE, AND WATER.

A Question of Time

You can't set a watch at the North Pole because it doesn't have an official time. The North and South Poles are the only places on Earth where all the time zones meet.

THE COLDER POLE

During the winter, the average temperature of the North Pole is about -30°F, but it's not the colder pole. That honor goes to the South Pole, with a record low of -117°F.

IN 1926, ROALD AMUNDSEN LED THE FIRST CONFIRMED EXPEDITION TO THE NORTH POLE USING AN AIRSHIP THAT NEVER LANDED.

In the summer, the temperature hits 32°F, the freezing point of water.

The NORTH POLE has exactly ONE SUNRISE (in March) and ONE SUNSET (in September) each year.

NO ONE KNEW FOR SURE IF THE NORTH POLE WAS ICE OR LAND UNTIL 1958, WHEN THE *NAUTILUS*, A US SUBMARINE, TRAVELED DIRECTLY UNDER THE SHEETS OF ICE.

NORTH POLE

Every April, runners race around the North Pole for the World's Coolest Marathon. First held in 2002 with only one runner, it has since attracted over 550 runners from over 50 nations.

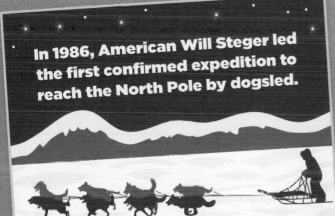

In 1986, American Will Steger led the first confirmed expedition to reach the North Pole by dogsled.

Get My Drift?

No one has ever lived on the North Pole. The ice moves too quickly for people to put up homes or build permanent research stations. Even polar bears avoid it.

Rulers of the Sea

WHALE TALK

Blue whales can communicate over thousands of miles. In theory, a whale in the Atlantic Ocean can "talk" to a whale in the Pacific!

SPERM WHALES GET THE LEAST SLEEP OF ANY ANIMAL, NAPPING FOR 12 MINUTES AT A TIME—LESS THAN TWO HOURS A DAY ALL TOGETHER.

The Greenland shark lives longer than any other vertebrate—an unbelievable 400 years.

IN 2017, THE UNITED STATES HAD 53 UNPROVOKED SHARK ATTACKS— THE MOST OF ANY COUNTRY IN THE WORLD—BUT NO FATALITIES.

BIG MOUTH BOWHEAD

The bowhead whale has the biggest mouth in the sea—and on land—at 16 feet long, 12 feet high, and 8 feet wide. Plus, its tongue weighs a ton—literally!

The great white shark is the only shark that can lift its head out of water to look for prey.

The enormous whale shark doesn't pursue any kind of prey; it just opens its mouth and swims.

A whale shark can have **300** pups at once.

There are more than 400 types of sharks, ranging from teeny tiny—the dwarf lantern shark is about 6½ inches—to the biggest fish in the world, the 45-foot whale shark.

What's for Dinner?

Sharks swallow all sorts of strange things. Chairs, shoes, license plates, and a drum set have all been found in their stomachs.

All About the Scouts

Girl Scouts

A REAL TROOP-ER

Juliette Gordon Low sold her jewelry so she could start the Girl Scouts of America. The first troop began with just 18 girls in Savannah, Georgia, on March 12, 1912.

In 1917, the Mistletoe Troop in Muskogee, Oklahoma, became the first to sell cookies—and a Girl Scout tradition was born.

The Girl Scouts were originally called Girl Guides.

Girls on the Go

In the 1940s, Girl Scout programs taught survival skills, along with airplane navigation and repair. Some scouts even earned pilot certificates.

Everyone Is Welcome

Inspired by Gordon Low, who was deaf, the Girl Scouts became one of the first youth organizations to welcome members with disabilities. In the 1930s, they published their materials in braille.

Who Was a Girl Scout?

Famous graduates include: Hillary Clinton, Michelle Obama, Sally Ride, Venus Williams, and Taylor Swift.

EACH YEAR, THE GIRL SCOUTS SELL AROUND 200 MILLION BOXES OF COOKIES, WORTH AROUND $800 MILLION. THIN MINTS ARE THE MOST POPULAR.

Boy Scouts

The original fee for Boy Scouts membership was 25 cents.

One Misty Moment

American newspaper publisher W.D. Boyce started the Boy Scouts of America in 1910 after a trip to England. Boyce got lost in a London fog and a Scout gave him directions, refusing any payment.

After writing a handbook for soldiers, British founder Robert Baden-Powell adapted the scouting book for younger readers, kick-starting the entire Boy Scout movement in 1908.

Animal Jamboree

The first World Scout Jamboree took place in 1920, with 8,000 Scouts from 34 countries, some bringing animals native to their regions—including an alligator from Florida and a lion cub from what is now Zimbabwe!

Scouts of Renown

Eleven of the 12 astronauts to walk on the moon were Boy Scouts. The Scouts have also included presidents: John F. Kennedy, Gerald Ford, Bill Clinton, and George W. Bush.

Beatle Scouts

John Lennon and Paul McCartney were both Boy Scouts, but McCartney really stuck with it. After he was invited to join Lennon's pre-Beatles band, he missed the first performance to go to Scout camp.

Barack Obama belonged to the Gerakan Pramuka, the Indonesian Scout Association, when he lived in the Southeast Asian country as a boy.

High in the Sky

How tall is a skyscraper? Experts say at least 40 floors, but in the future buildings will most likely be taller...and taller.

The Stories Begin

The first modern skyscraper was just 10 stories high and 138 feet tall: The Home Insurance Building, built in 1885 in Chicago, was demolished 46 years later, making way for a 45-story skyscraper that's still standing.

"SKYSCRAPER" ORIGINALLY MEANT A MAN OF GREAT HEIGHT, A TALL HAT, A LARGE HORSE, OR A TRIANGLE-SHAPED SAIL ON A SHIP.

HONG KONG HAS MORE THAN 300 SKYSCRAPERS, THE MOST OF ANY CITY IN THE WORLD.

In 2009, the Burj Khalifa in Dubai became the world's tallest building, standing 2,722 feet high—more than twice as tall as the Empire State Building.

GOING UP?

The fastest elevator in the world is in a Chinese skyscraper. Traveling at an incredible 45.8 miles per hour up and down the Shanghai Tower, it zips past all 127 floors in well under a minute.

Saudi Arabia's KINGDOM TOWER, also called the JEDDAH TOWER, is EXPECTED to become the TALLEST building on Earth, 568 feet HIGHER than Burj Khalifa.

Empire State of Mind

Completed in 1931 and standing 1,250 feet tall, the Empire State Building was the first skyscraper to go over 100 floors. With 73 elevators, 1,000 offices, approximately 21,000 workers, and its very own zip code, it was the world's tallest building for 40 years.

Skyscraper Day is celebrated every September 3.

Stormy Weather

The Empire State Building is struck by lightning around 23 times each year. During one incredible storm on April 12, 2011, it was hit eight times in 24 minutes.

Top Secret

HOW DID THE ARCHITECT OF THE CHRYSLER BUILDING MAKE SURE HIS SKYSCRAPER BECAME THE TALLEST OF ITS TIME? HE BUILT A SECRET SPIRE IN THE DOME, MAKING IT 1,046 FEET.

Founding Fathers: They Did Declare!

Switching Sides?

The Revolutionary War could have had a different ending. When George Washington was 14 years old, he wanted to join the British Navy, but his mom said no.

SIGNERS IN CHIEF

Only two future presidents of the United States signed the Declaration of Independence: John Adams and Thomas Jefferson. Both men died in 1826 on the very same day: the Fourth of July.

The Joker

Ben Franklin, a well-known author at the time, wasn't asked to draft the Declaration. Everyone thought he would try to sneak in a joke.

John Adams thought the president should be called "His Highness," "His Mightiness," or "His Elected Majesty."

Quite the Find

Around 200 copies of the Declaration were printed in 1776. One was discovered in 1989 behind a picture in an old frame and eventually sold for over $8 million. Dozens more could be floating around, so be on the lookout!

On the Wrong Side of the Law

STRANGE LAWS AROUND THE WORLD

In the United Kingdom, drivers are fined if they drive through puddles and spray pedestrians.

Legend has it that it was illegal to kill Bigfoot in 1800s British Columbia—although the locals referred to the creature as Sasquatch.

In Spain, drivers who wear glasses must always have an extra pair in the car.

Chewing gum or having gum on hand is banned in Singapore, unless you can prove that gum serves a therapeutic purpose.

Fishing for Trouble

Keeping a fish in a bowl purely for your own enjoyment is considered animal cruelty and is banned in Monza, Italy. If you're caught holding Bubbles hostage, you can be fined.

In order to buy a TV in South Africa, you need a license issued by the government.

Sneaking Around

Shh!

Sneakers are sneaky: The first rubber-soled shoes, called sand shoes, got their American nickname—sneakers—in the late 1800s, because they allowed people to move quickly and quietly.

He's an All-Star

Converse created one of the first basketball shoes—the All-Stars—in 1917. A sneaker salesman and player/manager of the Converse All-Star team was so dedicated to promoting basketball that, in 1932, the company named the shoe after him: Chuck Taylor All-Stars.

MOST PEOPLE IN THE UNITED STATES REFER TO THEIR ATHLETIC FOOTWEAR AS **TENNIS SHOES,**

WHILE THOSE IN THE NORTHEAST AND PARTS OF FLORIDA SAY **SNEAKERS—**

AND CHICAGOANS AND CINCINNATIANS CALL THEM **GYM SHOES.**

Reebok got its name from the South African spelling for the rhebok, a speedy African antelope.

NIKE WAS NAMED FOR THE GREEK GODDESS OF VICTORY.

Make a Swoosh

College student Carolyn Davidson designed the Nike "swoosh." She was paid only $35 at the time but continued to work for Nike. She later received 500 shares of the company—which are now worth more than $640,000!

In 1916, Keds designed the first sneaker for women, a high-heeled shoe made of canvas.

Do These Waffles Taste Funny?

In 1971, Nike cofounder Bill Bowerman was having breakfast when he realized that waffle-shaped grooves would be perfect for sneakers to grip any surface. Immediately, he poured a rubber mixture into the waffle iron to test it out, and the waffle sole shoe was born.

Tennis star Serena Williams wore sneakers to Prince Harry and Meghan Markle's royal wedding reception—paired with a floor-length gown!

Family Feud

How did the giant **sneaker** company **Puma** get its start? When **Adidas** cofounder **Rudolph Dassler** had a bitter **fight** with his **brother Adi**, he **left** the company to **start** another **brand**!

57

States of Mind

Meet at the Corner

It's possible to stand in four different states at the same time! Colorado, New Mexico, Utah, and Arizona all meet at one point, marked by the Four Corners Monument.

The Left Coast

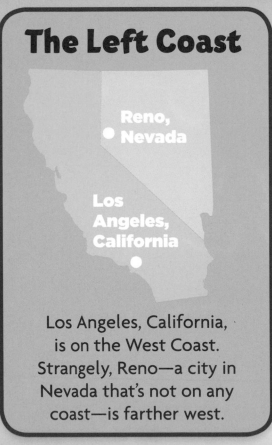

Reno, Nevada

Los Angeles, California

Los Angeles, California, is on the West Coast. Strangely, Reno—a city in Nevada that's not on any coast—is farther west.

TRAVEL ALERT

North America's driest, hottest region borders California and Nevada, has the lowest elevation on the continent, and gets only 2 inches of rain a year. It was named by 1890s Gold Rush travelers, hungry and thirsty as they headed west. Leaving the area, one traveler said, "Goodbye, Death Valley."

Far Out!

Alaska is farther north, east, and west than any other state. The state is so huge, it stretches all the way through the western hemisphere right into the eastern hemisphere.

A Greater Crater

What's the deepest lake in the United States? Crater Lake in Oregon, with a 1,943-foot depth, was created when a volcano broke apart almost 8,000 years ago, leaving a giant hole.

ANCIENT TREE-STORY

The oldest trees in the world are found in California's White Mountains. One bristlecone pine is believed to be more than 5,000 years old!

The Maine Effect

FREEZING COLD ESTCOURT STATION IN MAINE IS THE NORTHERNMOST TOWN ON THE EAST COAST. AMAZINGLY, IT'S FARTHER SOUTH THAN LONDON, PARIS, AND OTHER EUROPEAN CITIES WITH MILD TEMPERATURES.

A raindrop that falls into Minnesota's Lake Itasca, where the mighty Mississippi River begins, will take about three months to reach New Orleans, Louisiana, at the other end.

Island Hopping

During winter when the water freezes, you can walk from the United States to Russia. Two islands—Russia's Big Diomede and United States-owned Little Diomede—are only 2.4 miles apart!

Achoo!

Just one **SNEEZE** can spray **100,000 GERMS** into the air.

Kids get about three times as many colds as grown-ups.

There are more than 200 different cold-causing viruses—so many it's next to impossible for scientists to come up with a cure or vaccine.

One and Done

You never catch the same cold twice. Once you've been exposed to a cold virus, you're immune for the rest of your life. If only there weren't dozens and dozens more!

AMERICANS GET AROUND 1 BILLION COLDS EACH YEAR—FOR STUDENTS, THAT ADDS UP TO ABOUT 22 MILLION SICK DAYS FROM SCHOOL.

It's a Wash

Here's one way to stay healthy: Sing the "Happy Birthday" tune while you wash your hands. The song is 20 seconds long, the same amount of time it takes to kill germs.

IN 1997, MOUNTAIN CLIMBER ALAN HINKES—TRYING TO BREAK A SUMMITING RECORD AT PAKISTAN'S NANGA PARBET PEAK—SNEEZED SO HARD, HE INJURED HIS BACK AND HAD TO BE RESCUED BY HELICOPTER.

SNEEZE-A-THON

A 12-year-old English girl named Donna Griffiths started to sneeze on January 13, 1981, and didn't stop until September 16, 1983. That's 976 straight days, with approximately 1 million sneezes in just the first 12 months.

The average 75-year-old has had about 200 colds, spending two or so years feeling pretty miserable.

THE ACHOO BOO-BOO

When ancient Greeks caught a cold, they probably had bandages handy. Pricking patients to make them bleed was a common treatment.

A ROMAN PHILOSOPHER NAMED PLINY CAME UP WITH HIS OWN CURE FOR THE COMMON COLD: KISSING A MOUSE.

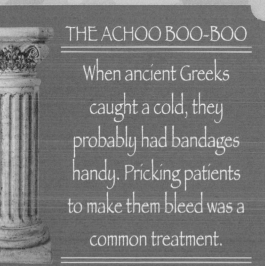

Doggone It!

According to the American Kennel Club, the Labrador retriever is the most popular dog breed—and has been since 1991.

Read My Wag

Dogs wag their tails in different ways for different reasons: Wagging to the right means they're happy, to the left means they're scared. Fast wagging may mean dogs are primed for action—ready to fight or run.

The Paw-fect Actor

German shepherd Rin Tin Tin was the star of more than a dozen movies in the 1920s. He received about 10,000 fan letters every week and was paid more than most human actors.

Puppy Love

George Washington was a true dog lover. He brought his dog Sweetlips to Philadelphia when he attended the Continental Congress, and when he found a lost dog wandering around a Revolutionary War battlefield, he quickly returned it to the owner, General William Howe, commanding officer of the British Army.

The basenji is the only dog that doesn't bark. It still makes noise, but it's more of a yodel.

Lightweight/ Heavyweight

The super-skinny greyhound is the fastest breed, running up to 45 miles per hour, while the English mastiff breaks a different record as the heaviest breed, usually weighing over 200 pounds. One mastiff registered a whopping 343 pounds on the scale!

In ancient times, Chinese royalty kept Pekingese guard dogs hidden in their long, flowing sleeves, ready to leap out to protect their owners.

Color-coded

If a dog has a dark-colored tongue, it's probably a chow chow or shar-pei. Most other breeds have pink tongues.

THE FRENCH POODLE ISN'T FROM FRANCE; THE BREED ORIGINATED IN GERMANY.

Celebrity Olympians

Royalty Rides High

Princess Anne rode into the 1976 Olympics as an equestrian, becoming the first member of the British royal family to compete in the Games. Her daughter, Zara Phillips, followed her lead in 2012 and won a silver medal in the sport. Her horse's name? High Kingdom!

Do You Know Judo?

Hilary Wolf does. She played the character of Kevin's older sister in the *Home Alone* movies, but she quit acting to concentrate on her real love, judo. A top-ranking athlete, she went to the 1996 and 2000 Olympics.

Baby expert Dr. Benjamin Spock won gold at the 1924 Olympics, rowing for the United States, before he exchanged dinghies for diapers.

IT RUNS IN THE FAMILY

Baseball star Jackie Robinson might have competed in the Olympics in track and field, just like his big brother, Mack Robinson, who won silver in the 200-meter race at the 1936 Berlin Olympics. Unfortunately, the 1940 Games were canceled because World War II had broken out.

On Stage and Slope

World-famous British violinist Vanessa-Mae competed in the 2014 Winter Olympics, representing Thailand. She participated in the Giant Slalom Alpine event and came in last.

WAR GAMES

In the 1912 Games, famed World War II general George S. Patton competed in the first modern pentathlon event. He finished fifth—strangely losing out in the shooting contest!

Word Scramble

At the Games

Unscramble the letters to spell the Olympic events.
Which event would you like to try?

EEPSD TINGSKA

_ _ _ _ _ _ _ _ _ _ _ _

OLEP LATUV

_ _ _ _ _ _ _ _ _ _

NASTYGMISC

_ _ _ _ _ _ _ _ _ _

CHABE BOLYLELVAL

_ _ _ _ _ _ _ _ _ _ _ _ _ _

EPIPLAHF OWNSDROAB

_ _ _ _ _ _ _ _ _ _ _ _ _ _ _ _ _

THALONRTI

_ _ _ _ _ _ _ _ _ _

TREWA LOOP

_ _ _ _ _ _ _ _ _

Under the Big Top

CIRCUS

is a Latin word meaning "ring" or "circle"—the shape of arenas in ancient Rome where chariot races and gladiator contests took place.

Funambulism is the art of tightrope-walking.

First President, First Circus

On April 3, 1793, the first circus debuted in the United States, thanks to a man named John Bill Ricketts. Two weeks later, George Washington sat ringside at the Philadelphia performance and was such a fan, Ricketts later performed at Washington's 65th birthday party.

LOAD 'EM UP

Have you ever seen a tiny clown car with 20 or so clowns jumping out and wondered how they all fit? The trick: The car is hollow, with the insides taken out.

When mistreatment of circus animals made worldwide news, Bolivia became the first country to outlaw their use.

Now the most famous circus in the world, Cirque du Soleil relies on arts like juggling, acrobatics, and stilt-walking, along with storytelling and music—no animals!

The word "leotard" came from Jules Leotard—the very first trapeze artist.

From 1968-1997, Ringling Brothers and Barnum & Bailey Circus had its own clown college, said to be harder to get into than any other school—including Harvard University.

JUST THEIR LUCK

Circus performers are known for being superstitious. Many make sure they step into the ring with their right foot, never wear green costumes, and avoid eating peanuts backstage.

RENT A TENT

The big top tradition began in 1825, when Joshua Purdy Brown had a great idea: Rent a tent and take the show on the road. His first stop was Wilmington, Delaware.

Silent Joey

In the early 1800s, Joseph Grimaldi became the first clown to use face paint and pantomime. To this day, silent clowns are called Joeys.

How Does Your Garden Grow?

The Biggest Bloom

The plant with the largest single flower is the *Rafflesia arnoldii* found in Indonesia. The bloom alone can be 3 feet across and weigh more than 20 pounds.

Some species of bamboo are gregarious—which means each and every flower in the same bamboo species blooms at the same exact time everywhere in the world.

Morning glories bloom in the morning;

moonflowers only bloom at night.

Good luck finding a four-leaf clover—the odds are 1 in 10,000.

In 1600s Holland, the tulip bulb became so valuable, just one was worth as much as a house—and more, some say, than gold!

Say It with Flowers

Floriography is the language of flowers, and in mid-1800s England it even had its own dictionary. People flipped through its pages to find out how to say "I'm sorry," "I love you," "good luck," and more, using flowers instead of words.

Worth the Wait

The tallest plant in the world, called the Queen of the Andes, doesn't flower until it reaches old age—anywhere from 80 to 150 years. When it does bloom, its 10,000 or so flowers bring its height to over 30 feet.

Veggies in a Vase

Broccoli may be your favorite vegetable, but it's really a flower. If left to grow, tiny yellow blossoms appear on the florets.

THE DEADLY VENUS FLYTRAP HAS SPLIT-SECOND REFLEXES, SNAPPING ITS LEAVES TOGETHER TO TRAP INSECTS AND EVEN SMALL FROGS IN UNDER A SECOND.

THE GAS PLANT, ALSO CALLED THE **BURNING BUSH,** GIVES OFF A LEMONY MIST THAT CAN BE IGNITED WITH A FLICK OF A MATCH.

Petal PU

Rare, large, and stinky—the unusual titan arum is also called the corpse flower. When the bloom first opens, it smells like a rotting carcass, and its flower alone can be 10 feet tall. In August 2016, 20,000 people lined up to see one titan arum bloom at the Chicago Botanic Garden.

All the Write Moves

BEATRIX POTTER, WRITER OF THE PETER RABBIT BOOKS, HAD HER VERY OWN PET BUNNY NAMED BENJAMIN BOUNCER.

THE VELVETEEN RABBIT AUTHOR MARGERY WILLIAMS ALSO WROTE A HORROR NOVEL FOR GROWNUPS ABOUT A WEREWOLF—AS DIFFERENT FROM THE BELOVED STUFFED ANIMAL AS YOU CAN GET!

Dr. Seuss Day is celebrated on Seuss's birthday, March 2, but the famous rhyming writer was never a doctor of any sort and his real name was Theodore Seuss Geisel.

Maurice Sendak originally sketched horses for his classic Where the Wild Things Are but realized he could draw monsters much better.

A favorite children's book is Pat the Bunny, but author Dorothy Kunhardt was also a historian known for writing books about ABRAHAM LINCOLN.

Diversity in Action

In the early 1960s, Ezra Jack Keats broke the color barrier in children's literature with his picture books about Peter, the black hero of *The Snowy Day*. A child of Polish-Jewish immigrant parents, Keats knew what it was like to feel like an outsider and wanted to include characters from all backgrounds.

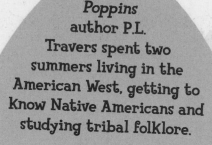

Mary Poppins author P.L. Travers spent two summers living in the American West, getting to know Native Americans and studying tribal folklore.

Shel Silverstein, famous for writing *A Light in the Attic*, *Where the Sidewalk Ends*, and other books, also wrote the hit song "A Boy Named Sue," recorded by country singer Johnny Cash.

Creative Sparks

While on a delayed train traveling to London in 1990, J.K. Rowling had an amazing idea, jotting down notes on a spare napkin that would turn into the Harry Potter series. *Goodnight Moon* author Margaret Wise Brown was skiing when inspiration hit. At the bottom of the mountain, she wrote the entire *Runaway Bunny* book on a ski receipt.

Harry Potter
Wizard
Magic school
Lightning scar

Ramona Rules

Beverly Cleary created Ramona when she realized every character in her Henry Huggins books was an only child. She quickly added a sister for Beezus, and the rest is kid lit history!

World Class

LONG LIVE THE KING

The King's School in Canterbury, England, is considered the oldest operating school in the world. Founded in 597 AD, it is still ranked as a top boarding school.

Boating Lessons

During Bangladesh's long rainy season, roads flooded so often that, in the past, children couldn't get to school. Now some students go to school-boats, floating classrooms that pick them up on riverbanks near their homes.

One school building in Germany looks like a giant cat, with two large round windows for eyes, a front entrance in the shape of a mouth, and a tail that's really a slide.

Start Here

In Holland, most children start school when they turn four—not on the first day of the school year. Students in Finland don't begin school until they are seven years old.

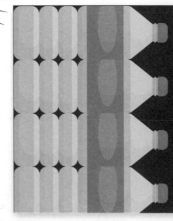

BOTTLES UP!

With help from environmentalists, a school in the Philippines was built using 9,000 recycled soda bottles. The bottles were filled with sand, water, and straw and stacked inside concrete frames to make the walls.

ZIP TRIP

For years, in an isolated valley in Colombia called Los Pinos, students took a zip line ride to school, crossing a steep canyon at 40 miles per hour. The only other route: trekking through the jungle on an hours-long hike each way.

SCRUB-A-SCHOOL

Japanese schools don't have custodians or janitors. Adult staff does some cleaning, but the students do the bulk of the work. Helping out with *o-soji*, or "the great cleaning," they are responsible for taking care of their own classrooms and other rooms as well.

HIGH SCHOOL

The elementary school in Phumachangtang, Tibet, on the slopes of the Himalayas, is thought to have the highest altitude of any school in the world. At about 17,628 feet in the air, it's even higher than the Mount Everest base camp.

1 September

A Jolly Knowledge Day

Russian schools always start on September 1st, no matter the day of the week. Why? It's a special holiday called The Day of Knowledge.

If you're a student in Chile, your summer vacation begins in December and ends in March; in the southern hemisphere, seasons are reversed.

In 2014, eight-year-old Sofia Viola was the only student to attend elementary school in the small town of Alpette, Italy, making it the smallest school ever.

CITY MONTESSORI SCHOOL IN LUCKNOW, INDIA, HOLDS THE RECORD FOR THE **BIGGEST** SCHOOL EVER, WITH 55,000 STUDENTS AGED FIVE TO 17, AND MORE THAN 1,000 CLASSROOMS.

Lady Liberty

The Statue of Liberty's official name is **Liberty Enlightening the World.**

Lady Liberty weighs **450,000 pounds,** and her **25-foot-long** feet wear **size 879** sandals.

SCULPTOR FREDERIC BARTHOLDI USED HIS MOM, CHARLOTTE, FOR A MODEL OF LADY LIBERTY'S 8-FOOT-TALL FACE.

There are **354 steps** from the statue's base to its crown, where visitors can look out 25 windows.

The statue, a gift from France, took nine years to build, with crews working around the clock, seven days a week.

A Crowning Achievement

The seven spikes on the crown are said to represent the seven oceans and seven continents—or seven rays of light. Each spike is about 9 feet long and weighs around 150 pounds.

At the time of its dedication, the Statue of Liberty was the tallest structure in New York City, 151 feet from the base to the torch.

Statue Silliness

When the statue arrived on Liberty Island, military families—along with a few others—were already living there. Sometimes children played inside Lady Liberty, dropping baseballs from its crown and rocking the torch.

Women were banned from the dedication ceremony, but—as a form of protest—one women's group held their own ceremony aboard a boat in New York harbor.

Body Parts

In 1878, Lady Liberty's head was displayed at the Paris World's Fair to raise money to complete the statue. The arm holding the torch was also shown in the United States a decade before the rest of the statue arrived.

BiTS AND PiECES

The fully constructed statue was presented to the United States in Paris on July 4, 1884, then taken apart and shipped across the Atlantic. The 214 crates contained 350 pieces that were put back together in New York.

Paper Route

New York's ticker-tape parade tradition—honoring sports teams, astronauts, and others—began on October 28, 1886, with a Statue of Liberty celebration. Workers unfurled long, winding tickers—papers with stock market information—from tall office windows as the parade passed by.

THE COPPER STATUE WAS ORIGINALLY THE COLOR OF A SHINY NEW PENNY, BUT AFTER 20 YEARS OR SO, IT TURNED GREEN BECAUSE OF ITS CHEMICAL REACTION WITH SEAWATER.

North Against South

THE NORTH'S UNION ARMY—WITH 2.1 MILLION SOLDIERS—WAS TWICE THE SIZE OF THE CONFEDERATE ARMY.

Called the Angel of the Battlefields, Clara Barton, a nurse for the Union Army, went on to found the American Red Cross.

One-third of Union soldiers were immigrants, and nearly 1 in 10 were African American.

At the time of the Civil War (1861-1865), around 9 million people lived in the South, and slaves made up almost one-third of the population.

TRAGIC TIMES

The Civil War was the deadliest war in American history, with about 625,000 fatalities. More than twice as many soldiers died from disease than were killed in action.

The Difference in Dollars

In 1863, black soldiers were finally allowed to fight for the Union. They earned $10 per month and had to rent their uniforms for $3 per month, while white soldiers earned at least $13 per month and received free uniforms.

MORE THAN HALF OF ALL BLACK UNION SOLDIERS WERE ESCAPED SLAVES.

Brother vs. Brother

Andrew and William Shriver lived in Union Mills, Maryland—a border state—just across the road from one another. Andrew owned slaves, yet he supported the North, while William had no slaves but was pro-South. The brothers didn't enlist, but their sons did, fighting for different sides.

AFTER SERVING AS THE FIRST FEMALE SURGEON IN MILITARY HISTORY, DR. MARY EDWARDS WALKER BECAME THE FIRST WOMAN TO RECEIVE THE CONGRESSIONAL MEDAL OF HONOR.

Two Men, One Name

Jefferson Davis was president of the Confederacy, but there was another Jefferson Davis, too—a general for the North. It caused great confusion at the Battle of Horseshoe Ridge, when Confederate men called out that they were Jeff Davis's troops and Union officers thought they were allies.

A MILITARY CEMETERY

When Confederate general Robert E. Lee's family fled their plantation, Northern troops used it for headquarters, setting aside a portion to bury the dead. Eventually, the entire piece of land became Arlington National Cemetery, with men and women buried from every war since the Revolution.

Just Saying

—an attempt that was almost successful—dates back to the mid-1900s when cigars were handed out as prizes at fairs and carnivals.

"Resting on one's laurels" —getting lazy because of past success—dates back to ancient Greece and the original Olympic Games, where winners received wreaths made of laurel branches.

Ax-idents Happen

If someone **"flies off the handle,"** he or she loses control. The phrase goes back to early farming days, when ax heads would come off during use.

THE PHRASE "BURY THE HATCHET" MEANS TO END A QUARREL OR CONFLICT, WITH ROOTS IN THE NATIVE AMERICAN TRADITION OF BURYING WEAPONS AS A SYMBOL OF PEACE.

Pain Refrain

During the Civil War, before pain medicine was available on the battlefield, it's believed that doctors tried to distract patients by telling them to bite down on a bullet. Today, when you "bite the bullet," you keep going no matter how difficult the situation.

Winds of Change

When you're "taken aback," you're surprised. The phrase comes from old sailing ships changing direction because of a sudden, unexpected shift of wind.

A Phrase of the Moon

When something happens "once in a blue moon," it means the event is very rare, just like a blue moon—the second full moon in one month. A blue moon only happens once every two to three years.

The phrase "saved by the bell" comes from boxing bouts, where a ringing bell signals the end of a round.

It's Better with Butter

There are two theories on how "butter someone up"—to flatter someone—came about: One theory says it came from an old Indian custom of tossing butter at statues of gods to seek favor, and another claims it was based on the simple act of spreading butter on a piece of bread to make it taste better.

In the 1950s, people began describing something bad or unpleasant as "the pits," using the slang term for armpit.

THE EXPRESSION "RAINING CATS AND DOGS" IS UNCERTAIN, BUT IT MAY HAVE COME FROM LONG AGO, WHEN PETS HID ON THATCHED ROOFS AND SLIPPED OFF IN HEAVY DOWNPOURS.

Everyone's Scared
of Something!

PSYCHOLOGISTS RECOGNIZE HUNDREDS OF DIFFERENT PHOBIAS, BUT THE ONE THAT TOPS MOST LISTS IS **ARACHNOPHOBIA,** OR FEAR OF **SPIDERS.**

IN ONE STUDY, THOSE SUFFERING FROM **ACROPHOBIA, OR FEAR** OF **HEIGHTS,** ESTIMATED BUILDINGS WERE 40 FEET TALLER THAN THEY TRULY WERE—BUT ONLY WHEN THEY STOOD ON THE ROOF.

PHOBIA is the **GREEK** word for **FEAR.**

More than **25%** of all people have **glossophobia,** the **fear** of **public speaking,** but in one way or another it affects up to **75%** of the population.

Crack the Code

Phobias

Don't be afraid to figure out this puzzle! Use the key at right to find out the official term for each fear.

1=H	5=G	9=Q	13=Z	17=S	21=L	25=C
2=M	6=O	10=D	14=F	18=Y	22=V	26=K
3=E	7=A	11=W	15=J	19=B	23=I	
4=P	8=T	12=N	16=U	20=X	24=R	

Astraphobia: fear of

8 1 16 12 10 3 24   7 12 10

21 23 5 1 8 12 23 12 5

Odontophobia: fear of going to the ___ ___ ___ ___ ___ ___ ___
10 3 12 8 23 17 8

Xanthophobia: fear of the ___ ___ ___ ___ ___
25 6 21 6 24

___ ___ ___ ___ ___ ___
18 3 21 21 6 11

Coulrophobia: fear of ___ ___ ___ ___ ___ ___
25 21 6 11 12 17

Turophobia: fear of ___ ___ ___ ___ ___ ___
25 1 3 3 17 3

Phobophobia: fear of having a

___ ___ ___ ___ ___ ___
4 1 6 19 23 7

Far-out Fashion

In the late 1700s and early 1800s, a specific shade of green was all the rage, and to get it, clothes had to be dyed with a poison called arsenic.

ARSENIC.
POISON

The Longer the Shoe. the Higher the Status

Imagine leather men's shoes with long pointed toes stretching up to 2 feet in front of the wearer, sometimes stuffed with hay and sometimes chained to the knee so the man could walk. What exactly are they? Crackowes or poulaines, fashionable footwear in the late 14th century.

Bustles were popular for women in the 1800s; these were cushions placed above the rear under dresses, puffing them out in the back.

Make Way for Women

Some styles in the 17th and 18th centuries were so bulky, women had to walk sideways to get through doors! Panniers were basketlike frames worn under dresses that made skirts stick out like shelves. Hoop skirts or crinolines were bell-shaped frames that pushed skirts up and out—so difficult to control in wind that women were blown off cliffs.

In the 1800s, women wore full-length dresses to swim at the beach, and though by the early 1900s the outfits grew shorter, stockings were still a must.

THANKS TO RAP STAR MC HAMMER, IT WAS TOTALLY COOL TO WEAR PARACHUTE PANTS IN THE EARLY 1990s.

Men and women wore corsets from the 1500s to the 1800s, girdle-like garments meant to shrink waistlines and stomachs, laced up and pulled so tightly, they caused indigestion, constipation, and worse!

UNTIL THE 1930s, MEN'S BATHING SUITS WERE MORE LIKE LONG UNDERWEAR.

The Art of the Matter

Starry Night Story

Vincent Van Gogh painted his most famous work, *Starry Night*, looking out of a hospital window while he was being treated for mental illness. Today, an entire wing of the hospital is a Van Gogh museum.

In 1961, **Henri Matisse's** painting **Le Bateau** hung **upside down** in **New York City's Museum of Modern Art** for **47 days**, until a visitor pointed out the **mistake.**

THE MISSING MASTERPIECE

The *Mona Lisa* was painted in 1507, but Leonardo Da Vinci's work first became famous in 1911, when it was stolen from the Louvre and made headline news around the world.

Georgia O'Keeffe, known for her New Mexico landscapes of the 1930s and '40s, rearranged the seats of her car to convert it into a mobile art studio so she could travel to the desert and paint.

In 1937, Spanish artist Pablo Picasso painted *Guernica*, a devastating scene of the Spanish city bombed by the Nazis, based on descriptions in a newspaper article.

THERE GO THE TOES

In 1495, when Da Vinci began painting *The Last Supper* directly on a wall in the Convent of Santa Maria delle Grazie in Milan, Italy, he included Jesus at the table—with feet. In 1652, workers installed a new doorway in the room and accidentally cut out the bottom of the mural—so now the feet are gone!

Celebrated impressionist **Claude Monet**, best known for paintings of his **pond full of water lilies** in Giverny, France, had a gardener paddle around to clean each and every lily pad.

In 2016, the Art Institute of Chicago recreated a room in the city to match Van Gogh's painting *The Bedroom* and rented it on Airbnb for $10 a night.

A COUPLE IN BRISTOL, ENGLAND, COULDN'T SELL THEIR HOUSE BECAUSE OF A LARGE MURAL ON ITS SIDE, PAINTED BY GRAFFITI ARTIST BANKSY—UNTIL THEY PUT THE MURAL ON THE MARKET AND SAID THE HOUSE WAS FREE!

Amazing Ant-ics

THERE ARE ABOUT 1 MILLION ANTS FOR EVERY HUMAN BEING ON EARTH.

Follow the Leader

An ant colony can't last without a *queen*. When one dies, the group dies out in a few months.

That's Gotta Hurt

The bullet ant—the largest ant in the world—gets its name from the strength of its sting, often compared to the force of a bullet and 30 times more powerful than a bee's sting. Luckily, this ant is only found in the rain forest and just uses its stinger for self-defense.

IN SOME PARTS OF THE WORLD, ANTS ARE A DELICACY SERVED IN FANCY RESTAURANTS.

Listen UP—or DOWN

ANTS DON'T HAVE EARS. THEY HEAR WITH THEIR FEET, FEELING VIBRATIONS IN THE GROUND.

Using Their Heads

The heads of some soldier ants are the exact same shape as the entrance to their nest. This way, they can block the opening by sitting close by and plugging up the empty space like a puzzle piece.

OPERATION: PROTECT THE NEST

In heavy rains, fire ants leap into action to keep the nest dry: They can form a tower 30 ants high or weave their bodies together to make a raft, capable of floating for weeks and weeks.

Ants have been around for 130 million years, surviving the meteor strike that most likely killed off the dinosaurs.

Worker ants take about 250 power naps every day—about one minute each—basically working 24-7.

HEAVY LIFTING

SOME ANTS CAN LIFT 20 TIMES THEIR OWN WEIGHT, SOME 50, BUT THE ASIAN WEAVER ANT TAKES THE PRIZE: IT'S CAPABLE OF LIFTING 100 TIMES ITS WEIGHT—THAT'S LIKE AN AVERAGE ADULT MALE LIFTING A GARBAGE TRUCK.

All worker ants—including soldiers—are female.

Women of the White House

Frances Colsom, the youngest First Lady, was only 21 years old when she married Grover Cleveland in 1886 and moved directly into the White House.

DOLLEY TO THE RESCUE

Dolley Madison saved George Washington—his portrait, to be exact. Just before British troops set the White House on fire during the War of 1812, the First Lady leapt into action and rescued a rare painting of the first president.

Herbert Hoover and his wife, Lou, were fluent in Mandarin Chinese and would often speak to each other in that language at the White House to discourage eavesdroppers.

Don't Forget About Us

Abigail Adams was all for equal rights. She famously told her husband John to "remember the ladies" when he helped create the Declaration of Independence.

JACKIE KENNEDY WAS THE ONLY FIRST LADY TO WIN AN EMMY, FOR HER 1962 TELEVISED TOUR OF THE WHITE HOUSE.

Called the "First Lady of Baseball," superfan Grace Coolidge cheered on the Washington Senators when her husband Calvin was president in the 1920s.

Flying High

On April 20, 1933, Eleanor Roosevelt left a formal White House dinner to fly with aviator legend Amelia Earhart. She rode shotgun but already had her own student pilot license.

Hillary Clinton was the first First Lady to later hold elected office and to be appointed to the president's cabinet as Secretary of State.

THREE FIRST LADIES WROTE BEST-SELLING BOOKS: BARBARA BUSH, HILLARY CLINTON, AND MICHELLE OBAMA.

On Screen

Ronald Reagan's wife Nancy starred in movies before she was First Lady. That's not so surprising: Ronald Reagan was an actor, too!

On Stage

Before she was First Lady, Betty Ford was a professional dancer. A member of the famous Martha Graham Dance Company, she performed at Carnegie Hall in 1938.

Touchdown!

ONE-STOP SHOPPING

All NFL footballs are made in the small town of Ada, Ohio. Three thousand footballs are finished each day, and they are the Wilson factory's only product.

The Baltimore Ravens' team name comes from a famous poem by Edgar Allan Poe, who is buried in the Maryland city.

And the Raven, never flitting, still is sitting, still is sitting...

Get Your Kicks

Football got its name from European soccer (called football, of course!): In the very first college game in 1869, players couldn't pick up the ball, only **kick it**.

In the early days of **PROFESSIONAL FOOTBALL**, Field goals **(FIVE POINTS)** were more important than touchdowns **(FOUR POINTS)**.

The 1972 Miami Dolphins, led by legendary coach Don Shula, is still the only team to have a complete perfect season—no losses or ties, including the Super Bowl.

New England Patriot **Tom Brady** has won **six Super Bowls**, the **most** of any **quarterback**.

Super Bowl Sunday is considered the second-biggest eating day of the year, ranked just after Thanksgiving.

And the Winner Is . . .

The Seattle Seahawks were named in a contest with more than 20,000 entries and close to 2,000 suggested names. Around 150 fans came up with "Seahawks," and they were each rewarded with tickets to a game.

SICK DAY

Walter Payton of the Chicago Bears broke the record for most rushing yards in a single game (275) on November 20, 1977, when he had the flu and didn't think he was going to play. His record held for 23 years.

Football on TV

Only about 500 people tuned in to the first televised football game on October 22, 1939. The matchup was between the Brooklyn Dodgers—who shared a home field with the baseball team—and the Philadelphia Eagles, and 13,000 people were in attendance in Brooklyn.

Capital Ideas

Tower of Power

When the Eiffel Tower was built for the 1889 Paris World's Fair, it was planned as a temporary structure. In fact, the tower was almost torn down in 1909, but officials realized it could be used for radio transmissions.

London, England, has 25,000 streets, and drivers who want to drive black cabs there need to memorize every road to pass a test called "The Knowledge."

Shop till You Drop

The Malaysian capital, Kuala Lumpur—the fashion center of the country—has more than 50 giant malls, including one of the largest in the world: the 7.5-million-square-foot Berjaya Times Square, with two luxury hotels, 1,000 shops, and more.

CAIRO, EGYPT, IS HOME TO THE ONLY REMAINING ANCIENT WONDER OF THE WORLD: THE GREAT PYRAMID OF GIZA, BUILT AROUND 2550 BC.

Fine Dining

You can find the oldest restaurant in the world in Madrid, Spain. Founded in 1725, Sobrino de Botín still uses its original oven—it hasn't been turned off for close to 300 years.

A Tribute to Laughter

The Cementerio General in Chile's capital has an area just for clowns—complete with a colorful big top, fake ticket office, and a sign that reads, "While there are children in the world, the circus will last forever."

WHEN THE 555-FOOT-TALL WASHINGTON MONUMENT OPENED IN WASHINGTON, D.C. IN 1884, IT WAS THE TALLEST STRUCTURE IN THE WORLD.

Next Stop, Russia

The Moscow subway system, with its arched ceilings, marble tiles, and chandeliers, is a tourist destination with guided tours and 44 stations named cultural heritage sites. It's easy to find your way while riding the train, too: A male voice announces stops going toward city center, a female announces them on the way out.

Denmark's most famous landmark—in the capital city of Copenhagen—is *The Little Mermaid* statue, inspired by Hans Christian Andersen's fairy tale.

The Subway Squeeze

More than 9 million people call Japan's capital home. It's no wonder Tokyo has *oshiya*—pushers—at subway stations to pack passengers onto already crowded trains.

© Pablo Hidalgo | Dreamstime.com

Spell-bound

"BOOKKEEPER" is the only word with **THREE DOUBLE LETTERS** in a row.

Strangely enough, many words related to the nose start with **"sn"**:

snout

sniff

snot

SNEEZE

Silence Isn't Olden

Sixty percent of words in the English language have silent letters. Centuries ago, those letters were sounded out, but over time pronunciations changed while spelling stayed the same.

"Angry" and "hungry" used to be the only two words that ended In **"gry,"** but now there is a third: **"hangry"**—for when you feel angry and hungry at once!

The word "alphabet" comes from the first two letters of the Greek alphabet, alpha and beta.

The J Way

Not one word in the English language ends with the letter J. That's because its sound is spelled out using "dge" as in "bridge" or "ge" as in "bandage."

There is only one word in the English language that begins and ends with "und":

"underground."

Fill in the Blanks

Every Letter Counts

There is a special kind of sentence that contains all **26** letters of the alphabet.

Fill in the missing letters below to complete the all-alphabet sentences. (Hint: If you're having trouble, look for letters that haven't been used.) Then write the numbered letters in order at the bottom of the page to find out what this type of sentence is called.

T___e quick brow___ fox jum___s over the l___zy do___ .

1   2

Ji___xed wizards pluc___ ivy from the bi___ quilt.

3   4

Six big juicy steaks si___ ___led in a pan as five wo___kmen left the quarry.

5

The five extremely bo___ing wiz___rds jump quickly.

6

Crazy Frederick ___ought ___any very exquisite opal je___els.

7

___ ___ ___ ___ ___ ___ ___

1 2 3 4 5 6 7

That's Old School!

The **oldest** public school in the *United States* is the **Boston Latin School,** which opened in 1635.

ATTENDANCE

DIDN'T COUNT

KIDS DIDN'T ALWAYS HAVE TO GO TO SCHOOL. IN THE 1600s AND 1700s, MOST CHILDREN IN THE SOUTH DIDN'T GO TO SCHOOL AT ALL; PRIVATE TUTORS CAME TO THEIR HOMES. IN 1852, MASSACHUSETTS BECAME THE FIRST STATE TO REQUIRE CHILDREN TO ATTEND SCHOOL.

In colonial times, certain towns allowed only boys to go to school, so some girls attended Dame Schools—run out of women's homes—where they were taught reading, writing, and household skills.

DIPLOMA

BY 1918, EVERY STATE REQUIRED STUDENTS TO GET AN EDUCATION—BUT ONLY THROUGH ELEMENTARY SCHOOL.

The Youngest Learners

The first kindergarten in the United States opened in Watertown, Wisconsin, in 1856, thanks to an immigrant teacher. Margarethe Schurz, who knew about *kindergarten* from her native Germany, used the same term, which means "a garden where children grow."

EARLY LEARNING

Teachers began using homemade blackboards in the early 1800s, sometimes coating pinewood with a mixture of eggs and burned potatoes.

GERM CENTRAL

During the 1800s, students didn't have water bottles or drink from fountains. Older boys went outside and filled a bucket with well water, and everyone drank from the same tin cup.

In the 1800s, no one was sent to the principal's office, because there was no principal. To discipline students, teachers rapped their knuckles with a ruler, had them hold a heavy book across their outstretched arms for an hour, or told them to sit in a corner wearing a cone-shaped dunce cap.

WHAT A CROWD!

Schools in the 1800s were usually one-room buildings, where one teacher taught all students, from grades one through eight. The youngest students were called abecedarians because they were learning their ABCs.

The **Supreme Court** case of **Brown v. Board** of Education outlawed **segregated schools** in **1954**, ruling that separate schools for **black** and white students was **unconstitutional**.

Don't Miss the Hack

In 1886, an Indiana company called Wayne Works made the first version of a school bus, a horse-drawn carriage called a school hack. Students had to climb in from the back so they wouldn't scare the horses.

Missions to the Moon

Why Flies?

Fruit flies were the first earthly creatures to launch into space, flying 66 miles up in 1967 to test their reaction to flight, since they are genetically very similar to humans.

ANIMALS in SPACE

DOGS, MONKEYS, AND MICE WERE LAUNCHED INTO SPACE WELL BEFORE HUMANS TO SEE THE EFFECTS OF ZERO GRAVITY. MANY DIED, INCLUDING THE MOST FAMOUS OF THEM ALL, LAIKA, A STRAY DOG PICKED UP FROM THE STREETS OF MOSCOW.

Man on Board

Russian cosmonaut Yuri Gagarin became the first human in space when he orbited Earth in 1961. Chosen for his pilot background and, some say, his 5'2" frame, he could easily fit inside the spacecraft.

To the Moon, but Not Back

In 1959, the very first spacecraft, Russia's *Luna 2*, blasted off for the moon. It was unmanned—a good thing, because it crash-landed as planned.

Astronauts have said that *moondust* smells like **gunpowder** and **wet ashes** in a **fireplace**.

What We Left Behind

After six moon landings, the moon is littered with leftover stuff, including three moon buggies, a photo of one astronaut's family, two golf balls, a small sculpture of an astronaut dedicated to the astronauts and cosmonauts who have died, and six American flags.

FOOTPRINTS FOR ETERNITY

Because the moon has no wind or water erosion, footprints left on the surface will be around a long, long time: according to NASA, "maybe almost as long as the moon itself lasts."

WHY WAS NEIL ARMSTRONG THE FIRST HUMAN TO WALK ON THE MOON IN 1969 INSTEAD OF BUZZ ALDRIN, THE OTHER ASTRONAUT IN THE CAPSULE? NASA STATES THE REASON WAS SIMPLE: HE WAS CLOSER TO THE DOOR.

Apollo 14's Alan Shepard snuck a golf club on board and managed to take some shots on the moon.

Panic on the Titanic

The luxury ocean liner *Titanic* sank on April 15, 1912, after hitting an iceberg on its very first voyage—despite the fact it was considered unsinkable.

TITANIC

At the time, the *Titanic* was the world's biggest ship—882 feet long—and the largest human-made moving object on Earth.

Could the ICE BERG

have been spotted earlier? The lookout binoculars were locked in a cabinet, and the key couldn't be found because the officer in charge had been replaced and never returned it.

Ice Strike

The ship set sail on April 10 from Southampton, England. A 100-foot-tall iceberg was spotted at 11:40 p.m. on April 14 by lookout Frederick Fleet who cried, "Iceberg, right ahead!" Thirty-seven seconds later, while trying to turn, the ship struck ice.

There were approximately **2,300** people on board, just over **700** survivors, and more than **1,500** deaths.

> Two or three small dogs survived the sinking of the Titanic.

Titanic Tickets for Sale

A team from the Woods Hole Oceanographic Institution discovered the shipwreck in 1985, 370 miles off the coast of Newfoundland. About 200 tourists visited the site—including one couple that married on the sunken deck, inside a submersible.

BOARDING PASS

DATE	CABIN CLASS	SEAT
11012019	PRIVATE	IL11

ADDITIONAL SEAT INFORMATION

What About the Lifeboats?

The *Titanic* had 16 wooden lifeboats along with four collapsible boats, enough space to hold about one-third of the people on board, but only if they were filled to capacity. Two of the boats were never launched.

Reel Life

Just weeks after the tragedy, the first *Titanic* movie was shown in theaters. A silent film called *Saved from the Titanic*, it starred Dorothy Gibson, an actress who had been on the ship. She wore the same clothes she had on the night of the disaster.

Mythical Monsters

YETI

Two Names, One Beast

The Yeti and the Abominable Snowman are one and the same: a hairy, apelike creature said to inhabit the Asian Himalayas. In 1921, the Yeti was described as a *metoh-kangmi*, or a "man-bear snowman," but a British reporter mixed up the translation, and somehow "man-bear" became "abominable."

License to Search

Stories of the Yeti date back to ancient Himalayan legends, but when a British explorer took photos of large, strange footprints in 1951, the entire world took notice. So many visitors flocked to the region, the government of Nepal issued Yeti-hunting licenses.

BIGFOOT SIGHTINGS HAVE OCCURRED IN ALL STATES EXCEPT HAWAII.

STARRING BIGFOOT

The most famous Bigfoot sighting took place in northern California in 1967, with actual film of a dark-haired creature wandering in the woods by Bluff Creek. The footage, captured by Roger Patterson and Robert Gimlin, can still be seen on YouTube.

Proof? Not Yet-i

OVER THE YEARS, SCIENTISTS HAVE STUDIED HAIR, TEETH, AND A FINGER SUPPOSEDLY BELONGING TO YETIS. EACH TIME, THEY CONCLUDED THAT THE SAMPLES WEREN'T REAL. THE JAWBONE WAS FROM A RARE BROWN BEAR, FOR INSTANCE, WHILE THE FINGER BELONGED TO A HUMAN.

The Chupacabra (translation: "goat sucker") was first reported in Puerto Rico in the mid-1990s, a seemingly alien being between 3 and 5 feet tall with a row of spikes down its back and vampire-like teeth.

Go to Google Street View, enter "Loch Ness," and you can search for Nessie yourself, looking above and below the water's surface.

The serpentlike Loch Ness Monster is said to live deep in the waters of Scotland's Loch Ness lake, with sightings recorded as far back as the 6th century.

Twister Time

In the **northern hemisphere**, tornadoes usually rotate **counterclockwise**, while in the **southern hemisphere**, they spin **clockwise**.

On March 21, 1932, a home was destroyed in Columbiana, Alabama, but somehow one table was left standing—with three dozen unbroken eggs still in place.

ABOUT **70%** OF **TORNADO WARNINGS** ARE **FALSE ALARMS.**

TORNADO

FOWL WEATHER

TORNADOES CAN BE DEADLY, TOSSING PEOPLE, CARS, AND BUILDINGS INTO THE AIR—BUT WHEN THE FEATHERS WERE BLOWN OFF 30 CHICKENS IN A LANSING, MICHIGAN, TORNADO ON JUNE 1, 1943, EACH AND EVERY ONE SURVIVED.

Tornado in a Bottle

Each year, over **2,000** twisters occur around the world, with three out of four touching down in the United States—the country with the most tornadoes worldwide. Without getting stuck in a tornado, you can get an idea of what a twister looks like by creating one yourself!

Make your own tornado, using these materials:

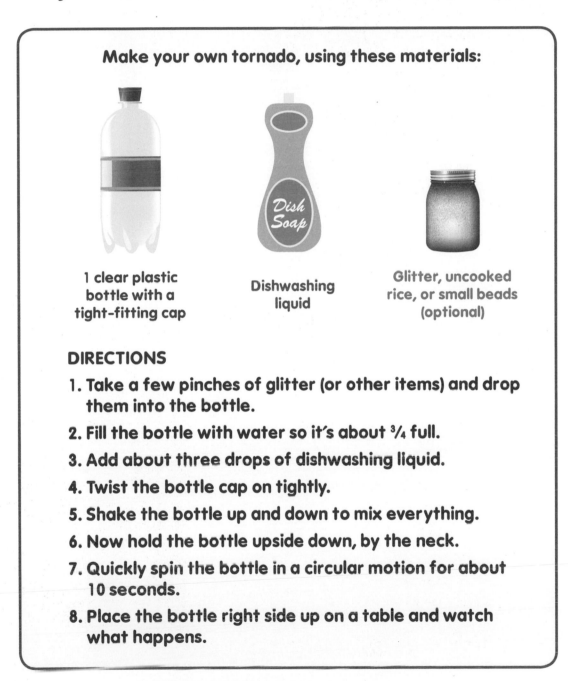

1 clear plastic bottle with a tight-fitting cap

Dishwashing liquid

Glitter, uncooked rice, or small beads (optional)

DIRECTIONS

1. Take a few pinches of glitter (or other items) and drop them into the bottle.

2. Fill the bottle with water so it's about ¾ full.

3. Add about three drops of dishwashing liquid.

4. Twist the bottle cap on tightly.

5. Shake the bottle up and down to mix everything.

6. Now hold the bottle upside down, by the neck.

7. Quickly spin the bottle in a circular motion for about 10 seconds.

8. Place the bottle right side up on a table and watch what happens.

You may need a few tries, but you'll see a funnel form a mini tornado in your very own home!

Down to Earth

Earth travels through space at about 67,000 miles per hour.

Since the moon rotates, people see only one side.

Out for a Spin

Earth's rotation is slowing down, but not so much that you would notice: just 2.5 milliseconds every century. In 180 million years, one day will be 25 hours long.

MILES TO GO

The longest known cave system on Earth is Mammoth Cave in Kentucky. Scientists believe it is over 600 miles long, but only 400 miles have been explored.

Rocky Record

The largest rock on Earth is in the Australian Outback. Mount Augustus is about 2,352 feet high—aboveground.

Lightning strikes Earth approximately 8 million times each day.

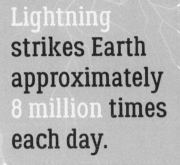

YOU CAN FIND THE **HIGHEST** WATERFALL IN THE **WORLD** IN **VENEZUELA.** **ANGEL FALLS** IS **3,212** FEET TALL, ABOUT THE HEIGHT OF A **300-STORY** BUILDING.

If you were to drop through the middle of Earth in a "gravity tunnel" it would take about 42 minutes to go from end to end.

ON THE BEACH

How many grains of sand are on Earth? Scientists say about 7 quintillion, 500 quadrillion—but of course no one's actually counted.

Animation Nation

FROM ZERO TO HERO

Toy Story's Woody wasn't always a heroic cowboy. He was originally a ventriloquist dummy—and a bad guy!

THE LION KING'S PUMBAA WAS THE FIRST DISNEY CHARACTER TO FART ON SCREEN.

HOW TO TRAIN YOUR DRAGON ANIMATORS WENT TO "FLIGHT SCHOOL"—A TRAINING CLASS ON **ANIMATED TAKEOFFS** AND **LANDINGS**—TO MASTER THE **MOVEMENTS** OF **FLYING.**

AND THE AWARDS GO TO ...

Snow White and the Seven Dwarfs was the first full-length animated movie with sound and color. When Walt Disney received an honorary Academy Award for its technical achievements, he took home eight Oscars—one regular-sized statue and seven smaller ones.

A Honey of a Movie

In 2017, one Netflix user streamed *Bee Movie* almost every day for an entire year. **Why?** It stopped her baby from crying.

TWO ♥ Twosomes

The actors who voiced Mickey and Minnie Mouse were real-life husband and wife. Wayne Allwine and Russi Taylor met on the job and were married for almost 20 years.

Frozen is the first animated Disney movie directed by a woman—*Wreck-It Ralph* writer Jennifer Lee, who later became Disney's chief creative officer.

Eve-Phone

Does Eve from *Wall-E* remind you of an electronic device you might find at home? Head Apple designer Jonathan Ives—credited with the iPod and iPhone—helped fashion her futuristic look.

©Tmyra | Dreamstime.com

109

Record Breakers

Big BOUNCING Ball

In 2018, credit for the biggest rubber band ball in the world went to American Joe Waul. Made of 7,000 bands and weighing over 900 pounds, the ball took Waul six years to complete.

APPLAUSE, APPLAUSE

Think you can clap fast? Try beating Seven Wade. He was nine years old when he broke the record for most claps in a minute: **1,080.**

Minoru Yoshida gets world record credit for nonstop pushups—all **10,507** of them in October 1980.

The Armless Archer

Matt Stutzman holds the record for longest accurate shot with a bow and arrow, standing **310** yards—almost three football fields—away from the target. Now consider this: The Paralympian athlete has no arms, so he shoots with his feet.

RECORD-SETTER EXTRAORDINAIRE

Ashrita Furman from Brooklyn, New York, holds the record for holding the most records. He set more than **600** records, including hula hooping on all seven continents and jumping up Mount Fuji with a pogo stick.

Rapid Rap

In 2013, rapper Eminem set the world record for most words in a hit single: **1,560** words in six minutes, four seconds. That's more than four words per second!

Shocking News

In a race to the finish, the speed of light would easily beat the speed of electricity traveling through a wire.

Birds rest on power lines and never feel shocks—unless they touch two different power lines at the same time and create a circuit.

IN 1882, THOMAS EDISON BUILT THE **WORLD'S FIRST POWER PLANT** IN NEW YORK.

An electric eel can produce five to six times more electricity than a household outlet.

If you use an average-sized lightning bolt to power a 100-watt light bulb, you can leave it on night and day for three straight months before it burns out.

Storm Safety

If your hair stands straight up during a storm, you'd better hurry indoors. It means lightning is about to strike—and you could be the target.

Pair Matching

Lightning Strikes

Draw a line to connect each lightning bolt on the left with its identical match on the right.

S-s-s-urprising S-s-s-nakes

"Snake Island" off the coast of Brazil has one snake per square foot—around 4,000 venemous golden lanceheads—so dangerous that it's against the law for anyone to go there.

A snake with its head cut off can be dead for hours but still deliver a poisonous bite.

MORE PEOPLE ARE KILLED BY BEES IN THE UNITED STATES THAN BY SNAKES.

After discovering snake skeletons wrapped around broken eggshells, researchers in India believe early snakes preyed on baby dinosaurs.

The deadly black mamba is the fastest snake in the world, moving at up to 12 miles per hour.

BIG MOUTH

Snakes can open their mouths so wide, they can swallow whole prey larger than they are. One python burst after trying to eat a big alligator meal!

When spitting cobras attack, they spray venom into enemy eyes; hitting targets more than 6 feet away, they are nearly 100% accurate.

No Escape

Snakes don't chew food, but many have rows and rows of teeth. Why? The teeth point backward to stop prey from crawling back out of their throats.

THE LARGEST SNAKE FOSSIL EVER FOUND— THE GIANT TITANOBOA—WAS DISCOVERED IN A COLOMBIAN JUNGLE, LIVED 60 MILLION YEARS AGO, MEASURED OVER 40 FEET LONG, AND WEIGHED MORE THAN 1 TON.

Size Doesn't Matter

A handful of animals are immune to poisonous snake bites. Hedgehogs, skunks, and even tiny woodrats can walk away unscathed.

Palindrome Fun

TOOT
KAYAK
RACE CAR

A **palindrome** is a word, sentence, number—or even a piece of music—that **reads** and **sounds** the same **forward** and **backward**.

The most recent **palindromic** year is 2002, and the next one won't happen until 2112.

Robert Schenkman, an American actor known for roles in 1990s TV shows, changed his name to make it a palindrome:

ROBERT TREBOR

In 1814, French emperor Napoleon Bonaparte gave up his throne and was exiled to an island called Elba, where, as legend has it, he said this famous palindrome:

"ABLE WAS I ERE I SAW ELBA."

PALINDROMES TO MAKE YOU LAUGH

Go hang a salami; I'm a lasagna hog.

Yo, banana boy!

Mr. Owl ate my metal worm.

Joseph Haydn's Symphony No. 47 in G is nicknamed "the Palindrome" because the second half of the piece is the same as the first but backward.

Car Talk

Radio Silence

Chevrolet came out with the first car radio in 1922. By the 1930s, some states tried to ban them, saying radios were too distracting for drivers.

On average, drivers leave their cars parked **95%** of the time.

THE DARK KNIGHT DRIVES

In two *Batman* movies, Bruce Wayne drives a Lamborghini Murciélago. *Murciélago* means "bat" in Spanish.

Not a Toy

The lowest car allowed to drive on roads is a student-made vehicle called the Mirai. Created in 2010 during an automobile engineering class at a Japanese high school, the car is only 17.79 inches high.

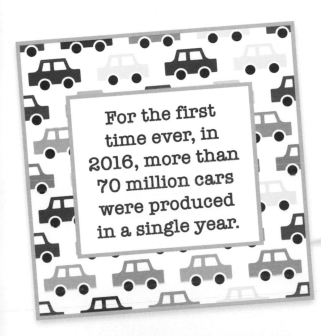

For the first time ever, in 2016, more than 70 million cars were produced in a single year.

In the Fast Lane

In 2010, a Swedish driver speeding through a Swiss village was issued the most expensive speeding ticket ever—$290,000. In Switzerland, the amount is based on the driver's income.

PEOPLE IN THE ARCTIC TOWN OF CHURCHILL, CANADA, ALWAYS LEAVE THEIR CAR DOORS UNLOCKED, IN CASE SOMEONE NEEDS TO JUMP IN QUICKLY TO HIDE FROM A POLAR BEAR.

You Can't Do That Here!
Wacky US Laws

License to Dress Up

There are laws governing high heels in Carmel, California. Fashion-conscious residents and visitors must get a special permit to wear shoes that have more than a 2-inch heel.

Secret Passwords

Be careful with your Netflix account in Tennessee. It's illegal for people to share passwords for music or movie streaming websites.

Whoever starts to sing the national anthem in a public place in Massachusetts needs to finish the whole song— people can be fined for stopping in the middle.

A MESSY ARREST

Visiting Gainesville, Florida? Then you'd better have plenty of napkins if you're ordering fried chicken. It's against the law to eat the southern favorite with anything other than your fingers!

DON'T RIDE A BICYCLE IN A SWIMMING POOL IN CALIFORNIA— IT'S AGAINST THE LAW.

According to state law, bingo games in North Carolina can't last more than five hours.

Two laws from Arizona don't seem to make sense: Children can't sing nursery rhymes after 8:00 p.m., and all camel hunting is illegal.

It used to be illegal to throw snowballs in Severance, Colorado, until nine-year-old Dane Best convinced town board members to strike the law from the books in December 2018—just in time for winter fun.

WEED THEM OUT

Watch out for dandelions in Pueblo, Colorado. It's illegal to let them grow in the city.

In New York, Georgia, and Alabama, you're not allowed to carry an ice-cream cone in your pocket on Sundays.

AR-kan-SAW

An Arkansas law declares that people must pronounce the state name correctly.

IN NEW HAMPSHIRE, IT'S ILLEGAL TO COLLECT SEAWEED AT NIGHT.

Lassie Laws

Illinois has some weird laws about dogs: In Galesburg, no one may keep a smelly dog. In Normal, it's against the law to make faces at passing pooches.

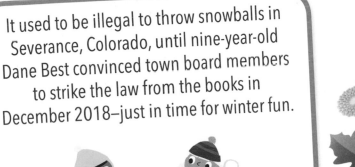

Search & Find®

New York City

New York City is one of the most culturally diverse cities in the world, with around 800 languages spoken by its more than 8 million residents.

Search & Find® these things that you might find around New York City:

 **Hot dog vendor**
 Jogger
 **Purple car**
 US flag
 Statue of Liberty
 **Bicyclist**
 Pizza slice

Answers on page 305

Get Out the Vote

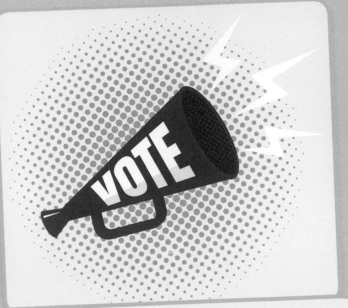

BEFORE THE REVOLUTIONARY WAR, VOTING TOOK PLACE AT LOCAL CARNIVALS, AND PEOPLE CALLED OUT THEIR VOTES TO BE COUNTED.

ELECTION DAY!

Why do Americans only vote on a Tuesday in early November for national elections? It's all about the farmers. The month didn't interfere with planting or harvesting, and since most farmers traveled long distances to vote, Tuesday was the most convenient day—with no church services or market days.

News Blackout

If people want to catch Election Day news or updates in New Zealand, they're out of luck. Reporters aren't allowed to cover candidates or give polling statistics until 7:00 p.m. that night to make sure voters aren't influenced by the media.

VOTE—OR ELSE

Twenty-two countries have mandatory voting, meaning their citizens are required to vote. If they don't, they may have to pay a fine.

Since 1977, astronauts can vote in space using a special electronic ballot—but only if they live in Texas.

Since 1944, Ohio has voted for the winner of every presidential election except for one: John F. Kennedy won in 1960, beating Ohio's choice of Richard Nixon.

Power to the Female

New Zealand became the first country to allow women to cast ballots in 1893. In Saudi Arabia, women didn't have the right to vote until 2015.

VOTE

THE NEVER-ENDING VOTE

Election Day can last a month in India. In fact, the 2014 election took over five weeks. With a possible 814 million people voting, and 900,000 polling stations, the system is too complicated to be any shorter.

That's the Ticket

Victoria Woodhull ran for president in 1872, almost 50 years before women were granted the right to vote. Her running mate was Frederick Douglass, the first African American ever nominated for vice president.

In some countries—like Brazil, Scotland, and Austria—you only have to be 16 to vote.

NEED YOUR VOTE

WON'T YOU BE MY NEIGHBOR?

Here's one way to become a citizen of Liechtenstein: Have your neighbors vote you in! Citizenship can be decided by a local election.

Fingers Crossed

For luck, tennis ace Serena Williams wears the same pair of socks for each game of a tournament, ties her shoes a special way, and bounces the ball exactly five times before her first serve.

© Zhukovsky | Dreamstime.com

JUSTIN BIEBER ONCE DYED HIS HAIR PLATINUM BLONDE, HOPING A NEW ALBUM WOULD GO PLATINUM, TOO.

Paris Hilton tries to make a wish every day at 11:11 a.m.

Game of Thrones star Kit Harington carries a lucky pen with him everywhere he goes—he's had it since he was little.

Early in her career, Ariana Grande made sure to eat a chocolate donut before every audition.

At least two celebrities make sure to step onto airplanes with their right feet first: Kim Kardashian and actress Jennifer Aniston.

Hair Cares

Only 1% to 2% of the world's population has red hair.

White Overnight?

A major shock can't turn your hair white. Once hair grows in, it doesn't change color.

HAIR LIES THE TRUTH

There's an entire science that can help police solve cases based on a single strand of hair. Forensic scientists analyze hair and provide information on suspects—what they look like, whether or not they were at the scene of the crime, and even what happened.

A STRAND OF HAIR CAN STRETCH 30% LONGER WHEN IT'S WET.

At any given moment, 90% of your hair is growing.

Hair loss can happen overnight, with a condition called alopecia areata.

One single hair will grow for about five years, then fall out.

Breathtaking Bridges

Power to the People

The lights on the Kurilpa Bridge in Brisbane, Australia, are powered by built-in solar panels. The bridge can supply power to the city, too!

Locks of Love

Couples visiting Paris used to snap padlocks with their names or initials on them onto the Pont des Arts footbridge and toss the keys into the river. By 2014, the approximately 700,000 "love locks" added so much weight to the bridge that part of it collapsed.

Bridge to Nowhere

The Half-Bridge of Hope is not a bridge at all—or even half of one. The wooden structure, tucked away in a small village in the Russian countryside, stands on a hillside, leads nowhere, and is really a piece of art.

THE WORLD'S OLDEST BRIDGE–A STONE ARCH IN IZMIR, TURKEY–WAS BUILT BY ANCIENT ROMANS AROUND 850 BC, ALMOST 3,000 YEARS AGO.

The Danyang-Kunshan Grand Bridge, part of China's railway system, is the longest bridge on Earth, spanning 102.4 miles.

The Bridge of Sighs in Venice, Italy, built in the early 1600s, got its name from prisoners who were led across it to the connecting jail, sighing as they walked.

Cross if You Dare

The Hussaini Hanging Bridge in Pakistan is one of the most dangerous bridges in the world. Made of ropes and walking planks placed far apart, the shaky bridge is too wide to hold onto both sides at once.

ON A CLEAR BRIDGE

The Zhangjiajie Glass Bridge, the world's longest glass-bottom bridge, allows you to look down into China's own Grand Canyon. At 1,410 feet in length, and almost invisible, the bridge proved so popular that officials placed an 8,000-person-per-day visitor limit.

© Rosana Scapinello | Dreamstime.com

Why Did the Rooster Cross the Brooklyn Bridge?

Because it's considered a symbol of victory! When the chief engineer fell ill while the bridge was being built, his wife, Emily Warren Roebling, took over his duties. She was the first to cross, in 1883, holding a rooster in her lap.

Walking through Water

The Moses Bridge in the Netherlands is named for the biblical Moses because it parts the waters. Constructed like a trench so it's hardly visible, the bridge allows visitors to walk below the water's surface.

Where Every Day Is Sun Day

The original meaning of the word "desert" is "an abandoned place."

SAND-ING TALL

Looking for the world's tallest sand dunes? Go to the Namib Desert in Namibia, where you'll see 900-foot dunes, plus Dune 7, which stretches 1,256 feet into the air.

Only 20% of deserts are covered by sand.

Considered the smallest desert in the world, the Carcross in Canada's Yukon Territory is only one square mile.

DRY GUYS

One area in Chile's Atacama Desert hasn't gotten rain in 500 years. It's the driest place on Earth where people live.

The Long Haul

In the late 1850s, the US imported camels to the Southwest to help army surveyors carry supplies between military outposts. The camel experiment ended with the Civil War. Most of the camels were auctioned off, but a few were found roaming in the Arizona desert for the next few decades.

The Heat Is On

The Sahara Desert in Northern Africa is the biggest hot desert in the world. It spans 11 different countries and measures about 3.5 million square miles.

Dinos in the Desert

In 1923, China's Gobi Desert turned out to be the site of one of the greatest dinosaur finds ever—eggs belonging to the meat-eating *Oviraptor*. Also found buried in the dunes: the first *Velociraptor* bones.

Snow Pants in the Sahara

You wouldn't expect to see snowfall in the Sahara, but it's snowed there three times between 1919 and 2018. The most recent snow lasted long enough to build snowmen and sled down dunes!

Every year, the wind blows more than 24 million tons of sand from the Sahara all the way across the Atlantic Ocean to the Amazon rain forest, where it helps plants grow.

AFRICANIZED HONEY BEES— BETTER KNOWN AS KILLER BEES—THRIVE IN DESERTS, BUZZING IN SWARMS OF 40,000 TO 100,000 BEES.

Kickin' It

Lionel Messi has never won a World Cup title for Argentina's national team, but he holds the record as the only player in soccer club history to score over 40 goals in nine straight seasons!

THE #1 SPORT

Soccer is the most popular sport in the world. More than 200 countries enter qualifications for the World Cup—the most watched sporting event on TV, with an audience of 3.5 billion!

Mighty Marta

Marta Viera da Silva is considered the greatest female soccer player of all time. As of 2019, she's been named FIFA player of the year a record six times and is the all-time leading scorer in the women's World Cup tournaments.

Soccer became the first Olympic team sport in 1908!

The United States won the first women's World Cup in 1991 and again in 1999, 2015, and 2019, becoming the only four-time champion to date.

Some sources trace modern soccer to prisoners in 1800s London who had their hands cut off for robbery and other crimes.

A BRIGHT IDEA

The first player to win three World Cups, Brazilian superstar Pelé is named after Thomas Edison, inventor of the light bulb. Pelé's real name is Edson Arantes do Nascimento.

© Jerry Coli | Dreamstime.com

FILLING IN

SOCCER is called "FOOTBALL" in every country except the United States, Canada, and Australia.

When soccer was dropped from the 1932 Olympics, the World Cup was created to fill the void. It was back in the program for the very next Games, but the World Cup continued.

On average, World Cup soccer players run about 7 miles each game.

FORMER CAPTAIN OF THE US NATIONAL TEAM, KRISTINE LILLY WAS THE FIRST WOMAN TO COMPETE IN FIVE WORLD CUPS.

© Oleh Dubyna | Dreamstime.com

Cristiano Ronaldo was the first player to score a goal in every single minute of game time.

Presidential Trivia

Simply Said

George Washington had the shortest inauguration speech ever. It clocked in at two minutes and was only 133 words long.

Statesman in Stitches

Andrew Johnson is the only president who never went to school. His family was so poor, he was sent to work for a tailor and always made his own suits.

Bear This in Mind

Thomas Jefferson kept two grizzly bears in cages on the White House lawn for a few months. They were a gift, and he needed to find them a home.

After hearing that president number 26, Theodore Roosevelt, refused to shoot a bear cub during a hunting trip, a toymaker named a stuffed animal after him: the teddy bear.

Lincoln on the Mat

Abraham Lincoln was a champion wrestler. He competed in 300 matches and lost only once in 12 years.

A Questionable Death

Twelfth president Zachary Taylor died in 1850. His body was dug up 141 years later to make sure he hadn't been poisoned. (It turned out he died from natural causes.)

Seventh president **Andrew Jackson** was in more than **100 duels.**

JAMES MADISON WAS THE SMALLEST PRESIDENT EVER, STANDING 5'4" AND WEIGHING ABOUT 100 POUNDS.

Cleveland Takes a Break

As of 2018, 15 presidents have been elected to two terms—but only Grover Cleveland didn't serve back-to-back. He was president number 22 and 24!

Presidents Barack Obama, Bill Clinton, and Jimmy Carter have all won Grammy Awards for Best Spoken Word Album.

HAIL TO THE CHIEF

William Howard Taft was the only president ever to serve as chief justice of the Supreme Court, appointed eight years after his presidency.

Rah, rah, sis, boom, bah: The 43rd president, George W. Bush, was head cheerleader at his high school Phillips Academy in Andover, Massachusetts.

When Barack Obama, the 44th president, lived in Indonesia as a child, he had a pet ape named Tata—as well as monitor lizards and a turtle!

The Bachelor

Only one president has never been married: James Buchanan, who served from 1857 to 1861. His niece stepped in as First Lady.

Jailhouse Rock:
Inside Alcatraz

Alcatraz is nicknamed "The Rock" because it was built on an island in San Francisco Bay that initially had little water or plants and was basically...

a rock!

Going, Going, Gone

Convicts spent a lot of time playing softball, with one major rule change: Balls hit over the fence weren't home runs. They were outs.

Notorious gangster Al Capone played the banjo in a prison band called the Rock Islanders until an unhappy band mate swung a saxophone at his head.

THIRTY-SIX MEN TRIED 14 DIFFERENT ESCAPES FROM ALCATRAZ; 23 WERE CAPTURED, EIGHT DIED DURING THEIR ATTEMPTS, AND FIVE WERE NEVER FOUND.

MOBSTER MEET-UP

Alcatraz was a gangster prison. George "Machine Gun" Kelly was there, along with Alvin Karpis, the leader of Ma Barker's gang of robbers and the last public enemy on the FBI's most wanted list to be captured.

TOURIST FOR A DAY

Infamous gangster Whitey Bulger was an inmate at Alcatraz in the early 1960s. In between prison stints, Bulger took an Alcatraz tour and had his picture taken with his girlfriend.

Just Like the 'Burbs

Families of prison workers lived on the island, too. There was a soda shop, bowling alley, pool tables, a grocery store, and a preschool. Convicts picked up the families' trash and did their laundry.

Today, top athletes compete in the annual Escape From Alcatraz Triathlon, which starts with a 1.5-mile swim off the island.

CONVICTED OF ARMED ROBBERY, FRANK WEATHERMAN WAS PRISONER NUMBER 1576, THE LAST INMATE SENT TO ALCATRAZ, AND THE LAST OFF THE ISLAND WHEN IT CLOSED.

US PENITENTIARY ALCATRAZ
1576
12 04 62

Costly Convicts

Alcatraz closed for one simple reason: It cost too much money. The island jail was three times more expensive than other prisons because everything had to be brought in, including close to 1 million gallons of water each week.

Protest with a Price Tag

In 1969, when the prison was already closed, about 100 Native American activists took over the island. They demanded the site be turned into a school and cultural center and offered to buy it for $24 in glass beads and red cloth—the same price their ancestors were paid for Manhattan in 1626.

Now part of the National Park System, Alcatraz gives prison tours to more than 1.4 million visitors every year.

★ ★ ★

Cereal-ly, Folks!

AMERICANS BUY AROUND 2.7 BILLION BOXES OF CEREAL EVERY YEAR.

Lucky Charms has just one original marshmallow shape left: the pink heart.

YOU'LL ONLY FIND COUNT CHOCULA, FRANKEN BERRY, AND BOO BERRY ON SUPERMARKET SHELVES AROUND HALLOWEEN, BUT WHEN THE "MONSTER CEREALS" FIRST CAME OUT IN THE EARLY 1970s, THEY WERE AVAILABLE IN WINTER, SPRING, AND SUMMER, TOO.

The word "cereal" originated from the Roman goddess of harvest and agriculture, Ceres.

In the 1950s, Katy the Kangaroo appeared on some Frosted Flakes boxes, Tony the Tiger on others, but the "G-r-r-r-eat" tiger outsold the kangaroo and became the official mascot.

One for the Rabbit

Trix may be for kids, but that silly rabbit finally got to eat an entire bowl—exactly once. In 1991, kids sent in box top "ballots" voting "Yes" the rabbit should get to eat his dream meal.

When they debuted in 1941, Cheerios were called Cheeri Oats, but Quaker Oats executives said it sounded too much like their company's name.

THE ORIGINAL TRIX CHARACTER WASN'T A RABBIT—IT WAS A FLAMINGO!

Thuri Ravenscroft, the man who voiced Tony the Tiger for Frosted Flakes, also sang "You're a Mean One, Mr. Grinch" in Dr. Seuss's *How the Grinch Stole Christmas*.

Beatlemania

A RICE HONEYS CEREAL BOX WITH BEATLES' YELLOW SUBMARINE RUB-ONS INSIDE CAN BE WORTH MORE THAN $1,000. ONE OF THOSE BOXES, PAIRED WITH A BEATLES WHEAT HONEYS BOX, REPORTEDLY SOLD FOR $11,000.

The Captain's Bio
Cap'n Crunch's full name is Horatio Magellan Crunch. He was born on Crunch Island, located in the Sea of Milk.

A CRUNCHY CASE

In 2009, a California woman took Cap'n Crunch to court, claiming Crunch Berries commercials tricked people into thinking they were getting real fruit. The judge threw out the case, saying customers knew Crunch Berries didn't grow on bushes.

THE FOURTH ELF

Brothers Snap, Crackle, and Pop once had a friend. In the early 1950s, Rice Krispies also featured a space elf called

POW.

In Living Color

Two-Tone Tiff

In 2015, a picture of a dress blew up the Internet: Was it blue and black or white and gold? People were divided, but it all came down to how their brains interpreted the background light in the photo. In person, it was blue and black.

GREEN SCHEME

US paper money has been green since 1929. The durable green dye was first used to stop counterfeiters, who had to work with black-and-white cameras.

In ancient Rome, only emperors could wear the color purple.

Colorful Translation

One of Russia's most famous landmarks, Red Square has nothing to do with the color. At one point the Russian word for red, *krasni*, also meant "beautiful."

When you picture diamonds, you probably don't think of the color brown, but chocolate diamonds are the most common type of the naturally occurring gems.

A Carrot of a Different Color

Until the 17th century, carrots were purple. Dutch farmers first created the orange carrot—some say to honor William of Orange, who led the Netherlands to independence.

Eating vegetables can change the color of your urine—try asparagus for a shade of green, or beets to turn pee pink.

The University of Iowa's football team welcomes opponents with a pink visitors' locker room, designed to lull players into a calm, nonaggressive state.

In Latin America, wearing YELLOW underwear on NEW YEAR'S EVE is thought to bring GOOD LUCK.

That Yellow-Red Fruit

Was the fruit named after the color, or the color after the fruit? The citrus treat was named "orange" in the 1300s, and the color—previously called "yellow-red"—followed about 200 years later.

The Bride Wore Green

Brides never wore white wedding gowns in England, the United States, and other Western countries until the mid-1800s. They preferred all different colors—even red—but once England's Queen Victoria wore a simple white dress in 1840, the new tradition took hold.

THE NEW BLUE

The Crayola crayon color Bluetiful, introduced in 2017, was based on the first new blue pigment in more than 200 years. The hue was discovered by a team at Oregon State University, mixing chemicals to manufacture electronic materials.

Come Join the Band

Former Beatle Ringo Starr developed his famously unique drumming style because he's a lefty and uses a right-handed drum kit.

Tiny Tunes

Made in 2009 by Chinese violinist Chen Lianzhi, the world's smallest violin measures less than ½ inch and has every feature of a regular-sized one. It can actually play music!

Slaves in the US South played drums to communicate in secret code, sending messages from plantation to plantation.

Violin strings used to be made from dried animal intestines, usually belonging to sheep.

In 1969, country music legend Willie Nelson ran into his burning house to save his guitar.

DEAF JAM

When Beethoven was going deaf, he didn't stop composing. It's said that he had two tricks to "hear": One trick was to clench a stick in his teeth, placing the other end on piano keys to pick up sound, and the other involved cutting the legs off his piano to feel vibrations on the floor and match them to notes.

British musician Jayson Brinkler played a single drum roll for 12 hours, five minutes, and five seconds to break the world record in 2015—then went straight to the hospital with an injured wrist.

VEGGIE NOTES

Musicians from the Vegetable Orchestra of Vienna shop at the supermarket before every concert. They hollow out carrots for flutes, make trumpets out of red peppers, and pound on pumpkins to assemble a drum set.

Name Change

The word "piano" is a nickname for the instrument. Its full name is **PIANOFORTE.**

In 1961, when people of color weren't allowed to join country clubs or go to "whites only" amusement parks, rock 'n' roll legend Chuck Berry built his own amusement park in Missouri, complete with a guitar-shaped pool.

SONG STREET

One road in California is really a musical instrument, built with special grooves that make a melody as cars drive on it. Keep to the speed limit, and it sounds like the "William Tell Overture."

Inventive Mistakes

As one legend has it, a resort chef was preparing French fries when a customer complained they were "too thick and soggy," so the chef cut the potatoes paper-thin, over-fried them, and added salt—creating the first potato chip.

Sweet Results

After a day's work in Johns Hopkins University's chemistry lab, scientist Constantin Fahlberg went home for dinner and, upon biting into a roll, thought it tasted extremely sweet. He realized he had leftover chemicals on his hands and hurried back to the lab to see which chemical caused the change in taste. Fahlberg, along with collaborator Ira Remsen, isolated the chemical and created the first alternative to cane sugar: saccharine.

A PERFECT CONE-COCTION

Ice-cream vendor Italo Marchiony invented the ice-cream cone in 1903 to replace the glass dishes he used to give customers—but the cone really took off at the 1904 World's Fair when he teamed up with pastry maker Ernest A. Hamwi, whose own waffle-like treats were rolled into cones to keep up with customer demand.

Sticky Situations

Dr. Spence Silver, a scientist at 3M, invented a unique semipermanent adhesive, but his company could not figure out how to put it to good use. Years later, fellow scientist Art Fry couldn't get his bookmark to stay in his choral hymn book. On a whim he decided to test Silver's glue as a way to get the paper to stick, and what started as a bookmark eventually became the Post-it Note.

KEEPING PACE

In 1950, Wilson Greatbatch was working on a device to record heart sounds when he pulled the wrong size resistor out of the box. The resistor gave off a rhythmic electrical pulse that Greatbatch knew could be used to replicate a human heart: the first pacemaker.

Street Smarts

Twisted Directions

Tourists flock to the crooked part of Lombard Street in San Francisco, which swoops narrowly back-and-forth eight times with a speed limit of 5 miles per hour. The street was designed because of the area's steep incline.

On the Up and Up

City planners in Dunedin, New Zealand, designed their street system as a grid before realizing that one area in particular had an extremely steep incline. Rather than change their entire plan, they pushed ahead and created Baldwin Street: the world's steepest street.

The world's oldest paved road served as a roadway between a quarry and a waterway in ancient Egypt and dates back over 4,600 years.

The United States is home to some wacky street names, including: Bad Route Road in Montana, Memory Lane in Mississippi, Chicken Dinner Road in Idaho, and Texas's Hairy Man Road.

MEMORY LN

The Straight and Narrow

Parliament Street in England dates back to the 14th century and is one of the world's narrowest streets. At its narrowest, it is about 25 inches wide—around the same size as a woman's footstep!

EYES ON THE ROAD

The Guoliang Tunnel in China, which connects the remote Guoliang Village with the rest of civilization, was dug by hand through a mountainside. The narrow tunnel is full of twists and turns, but windows cut into the rock allow drivers to look out at the stunning landscape and huge drop below.

Let the Games Begin!

FUNNY BONE
OS DU COUDE

WISH BONE
FOURCHETTE

BROKEN HEART
COEUR BRISÉ

ADAM'S APPLE
POMME D'ADAM

WRITER'S CRAMP
CRAMPE D'ÉCRIVAIN

SPARE RIBS
CÔTELETTES

BUTTERFLIES IN STOMACH
PAPILLONS DANS L'ESTOMAC

BREAD BASKET
BEDAINE

CHARLIE HORSE
CRAMPE DE CAVALIER

WATER ON THE KNEE
EAU DANS LE GENOU

ANKLEBONE CONNECTED TO THE KNEE BONE
CHEVILLE RELIÉE AU GENOU

WRENCHED ANKLE
CHEVILLE FOULÉE

The Doctor Is In

John Spinello was a college student when he created Operation for a homework assignment. He sold the game to a toy company for $500 and the promise of a job when he graduated. The game went on to be a classic, earning millions, but Spinello never did get that job.

The name "Jenga" is thought to be based on a Swahili word meaning "to build."

A professor named Erno Rubik designed the Rubik's cube in 1974 to help his students understand three-dimensional geometry, but the first time he mixed up the colors, it took him a month to figure out how to solve his own puzzle.

The Sweetest Game

While recovering from polio in a San Diego hospital, retired schoolteacher Eleanor Abbott invented Candy Land for the children on her floor. It became one of the most popular games ever—selling 1 million boxes each year. Abbott donated her earnings to children's charities.

In Scrabble, using all your letters in one turn is called a Bingo.

In Connect 4, there are nearly 2 trillion ways to get four discs in a row, and your chances of winning are improved if you go first and play the center column.

In 2016, the makers of Clue "killed off" old-fashioned housekeeper Mrs. White and updated her with another female suspect named Dr. Orchid, a poisonous plants scientist and the first character of color.

When Mr. Potato Head debuted in 1952, kids had to supply their own potatoes.

YAHTZEE was invented by a wealthy Canadian couple who liked to play the dice game on their yacht—hence the name.

A Trivial Case

In 1984, Fred L. Worth sued the creators of Trivial Pursuit, claiming that 25% of the game's questions were taken from his books. The judge ruled that no one can own facts, so Worth lost his case.

THE GAME CRANIUM WAS THE FIRST NON-COFFEE ITEM OFFERED AT STARBUCKS.

The longest chess game possible can take more than

5,870 moves.

Search & Find®

Rain Forest Expedition

The Amazon rain forest is home to about 40,000 different species of plants, more than 1,300 bird species, 430 different types of mammals, and at least 2.5 million kinds of insects.

Search & Find® these creatures in the rain forest:

Macaw Lemur Parakeet Leopard Flamingo Monkey Frog

Globetrotter

Canada has about 60% of all the natural lakes in the world.

Down In the Ocean Depths

At 29,029 feet, Mount Everest is the tallest mountain on Earth, yet it could fit inside the Marianas Trench—the deepest part of the Pacific Ocean. The trench measures 36,201 feet deep.

AFRICA IS THE ONLY CONTINENT THAT'S PART OF ALL FOUR HEMISPHERES— NORTH, SOUTH, EAST, AND WEST.

It may be one of the seven continents, but Antarctica is the only landmass in the world that doesn't belong to any country—at least officially!

Vatican City is 0.2 square miles, making it the smallest country—even tinier than the island of Manhattan in New York!

ICY HOT

Iceland has around 130 volcanoes and, on average, one eruption every five years. It has more than 260 glaciers, too. No wonder it's called the Land of Fire and Ice!

A BIG DEAL

Russia is the biggest country. It's more than 6.6 million square miles, nearly twice the size of Canada, and has nine different time zones!

The Amazon rain forest in South America produces almost a quarter of the world's oxygen.

ONLY THREE COUNTRIES IN THE WORLD ARE COMPLETELY SURROUNDED BY ANOTHER COUNTRY: SAN MARINA AND VATICAN CITY IN ITALY AND LESOTHO IN SOUTH AFRICA.

Strait News

Istanbul is the only city located on two continents. The Bosporus Strait runs through the Turkish capital, and it also forms a natural border between Europe and Asia.

CALL IT A TIE

Experts can't agree about the world's longest river. Some say it's the Nile, running through 11 African countries, while others claim that South America's Amazon should get the title. Both are around 4,000 miles long, but it's hard to tell exactly where they begin and end.

What a Crazy Bunch!

A group of owls is called a parliament, like the British version of Congress.

When butterflies flutter together, they make a kaleidoscope.

GIRAFFES TOWER OVER OTHER ANIMALS, AND THAT'S EXACTLY WHAT YOU CALL A GROUP OF THESE TALL MAMMALS—A TOWER!

Rhinos getting together? Call them a **CRASH!**

APES GATHER IN A SHREWDNESS.

OTTERS FLOAT TOGETHER IN A RAFT, WHILE SHARKS SWIM IN A SHIVER.

Squirrels hang out in a scurry—and they move that way, too!

Hedgehogs meet up in a prickle.

A bunch of ferrets is a business.

A group of **geese** on the ground is a **gaggle**, but up in the air geese form a **wedge**, **skein**, or **team**.

A group of crows is called a murder.

FOXES RUN IN PACKS CALLED SKULKS.

A sloth isn't just an animal; it's also the name for a bunch of bears.

What's a zeal or dazzle? A group of zebras!

Pandas form an embarrassment.

You can call a group of camels a herd, or you can call them a caravan!

Hoops, There It Is!

A New Game

In December 1881, James Naismith came up with the game of "basket ball" when he nailed two peach baskets 10 feet off the ground at either end of a Springfield, Massachusetts, gym. There were no basketballs back then, so the players used a soccer ball.

THE SACRAMENTO KINGS AND THE ORLANDO MAGIC HAVE BOTH RETIRED THE NUMBER 6—NOT TO HONOR ANY PLAYER, BUT TO THANK THEIR FANS, CONSIDERED THE "SIXTH MAN" ON EACH TEAM.

SIXTH MAN

6

IN THE VERY FIRST GAMES, PLAYERS WEREN'T ALLOWED TO DRIBBLE.

EACH NBA BASKETBALL HAS ABOUT 4,118 BUMPS CALLED PEBBLES ON ITS SURFACE, MAKING FOR EASIER GRIPPING.

The Long and

7'7"

Short of It

5'3"

The shortest NBA player ever is Muggsy Bogues, at 5'3". In the 1987–1988 season, he teamed up with 7'7" Manute Bol—co-record-holder for tallest player—on the Washington Bullets.

Lebron James is a **lefty**, but he shoots with his **right hand**.

Lebron James and Michael Jordan are the only NBA players to win League MVP, Finals MVP, and Olympic gold—all in the same year.

On Again, Off Again

Basketball great Michael Jordan retired from basketball three times! In 1993, he left his Chicago team to play Minor League Baseball for the White Sox. After returning to the Bulls, he retired—again— in 1999, only to wind up playing for the Washington Wizards. Finally, in 2003, he retired for the third and final time.

AN EVEN HUNDRED

Wilt "the Stilt" Chamberlain holds the record for most points scored in any one game. When his Philadelphia team played the New York Knicks on March 2, 1962, the 7'1" center collected an unbelievable 100 points.

THE CLEVELAND CAVALIERS (2010-11) and the PHILADELPHIA 76ERS (2013-14) are TIED for a record no team wants: longest LOSING STREAK in a season, WITH 26 GAMES.

100

On December 13, 1983, the Detroit Pistons beat the Denver Nuggets 186-184 after triple overtime—making it the highest scoring NBA game ever.

Long Distance Runner

NBA players run an average of **2.9 miles** in each game, with Portland Trail Blazer CJ McCollum logging in the longest distance for three straight years. In the 2017-2018 season, he ran **215 miles**!

Whiz Kids

A Talent for Drama

Famous composers Erich Wolfgang Korngold and Wolfgang Amadeus Mozart share a name and a major childhood accomplishment: Both wrote their first operas at the age of 12—Korngold in 1909 and Mozart centuries earlier!

IN 1994,

MICHAEL KEARNEY
YOUNGEST COLLEGE GRADUATE
EVER AT THE AGE OF **10.**

Chill Out

California native Frank Epperson invented the Popsicle® by accident when he was 11 years old, after he left a soft drink outside on a cold night in 1905. He called his creation the "Eppsicle," but by the time he got a patent in 1923, his own children were calling it "Pop's 'sicle."

ELISABETH ANISIMOW began selling "LIVING PAINTINGS"—artwork in which Anisimow paints living, breathing people, sets, and props to look like IMPRESSIONIST paintings—when she was NINE YEARS OLD.

Thinking Ahead

Dafne Almazán became the world's youngest psychologist in 2015, at 13 years old, beating her brother's record (16 years of age). The young Latina didn't stop there: In 2017, she became the youngest person to get a master's degree in psychology.

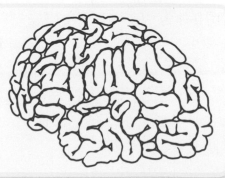

Tatum O'Neal became the youngest Academy Award winner at 10 years old in 1973 for Best Supporting Actress in *Paper Moon*.

ALL EARS

At age 15, American Chester Greenwood wanted to be able to ice skate outdoors without his ears freezing. The solution? He created a wire headband with loops over the ears, to which his grandmother sewed fur and velvet: the world's first earmuffs!

Quvenzhané Wallis, who was just six years old when she filmed *Beasts of the Southern Wild* in 2012, became the youngest Best Actress nominee for an Academy Award at age nine.

HUNGARIAN JUDIT POLGAR, LARGELY CONSIDERED THE GREATEST FEMALE CHESS PLAYER OF ALL TIME, WAS ONLY NINE YEARS OLD WHEN SHE FIRST WON AN INTERNATIONAL CHESS TOURNAMENT.

Indian American Tanishq Abraham, who earned three associate degrees by the time he was 11, was the youngest person ever to speak at a NASA (National Aeronautics and Space Administration) conference— at the age of nine!

Read All About It

More Is More

Some authors don't worry about wasting their words: Victor Hugo's *Les Miserables* boasts an **823-word sentence,** and James Joyce's *Ulysses* has a sentence with a whopping **4,391 words.**

Virginia Woolf's older sister, Vanessa Bell, designed the covers of all but one of Woolf's books.

The aroma from a book comes from the slow deterioration of paper over time and the release of fragrant chemicals like vanillin, which is why older books generally smell better.

Just One More Page...

Is it possible to read too much? American humorist H.L. Mencken thought so, and he coined the term "bibliobibuli" to describe people who do just that.

It's Raining Books

Iceland publishes more books per capita than any other nation. In fact, people in Iceland exchange books on Christmas Eve and then spend the evening reading and eating chocolate. This cozy tradition happens during a season known as Jolabokaflod, or "The Christmas Book Flood."

You're a Wizard, Elvis

The Harry Potter books have sold over 500 million copies worldwide and have been translated into over 80 languages. In each language, Tom Marvolo Riddle needed a different name so the letters would rearrange to say "I am Lord Voldemort." In the French version, to spell out "*Je suis* Voldemort," the evil wizard's middle name is...Elvis.

The most read book in the world by far is *The Holy Bible*, followed by *Quotations from Chairman Mao Tse-Tung* and the Harry Potter series.

President Theodore Roosevelt read an average of one book per day.

Mark Twain's *The Adventures of Tom Sawyer* was the first book written on a typewriter.

THE MOST EXPENSIVE BOOK EVER SOLD WAS *CODEX LEICESTER*, BY LEONARDO DA VINCI. BILL GATES PAID $30.8 MILLION FOR THE MANUSCRIPT AT AUCTION.

In the Middle Ages, books were rare and considered extremely valuable, so early libraries chained their books to shelves.

Down the Rabbit Hole

ALICE IN WONDERLAND WAS BASED ON A 10-YEAR-OLD GIRL NAMED ALICE LIDDELL. AUTHOR LEWIS CARROLL, WHOSE REAL NAME WAS CHARLES DODGSON, WAS A MATH PROFESSOR AT OXFORD WHO TOLD THE WHIMSICAL STORY TO ALICE AND HER SISTERS ON A BOATING TRIP. ALICE ASKED HIM TO WRITE THE STORY DOWN, AND THE REST IS HISTORY.

Greetings Around the Globe

SHAKE ON IT

In the Middle East, only the right hand is used in a handshake. The left hand is thought to be unclean.

IF YOU VISIT GERMANY, KEEP YOUR HANDSHAKE TO ONE FIRM DOWNWARD MOTION.

When going in for a handshake in China, loosen your grip.

BOW DO YOU DO?

In Japan, a bow will do to say hello. Just make sure it's the right kind: There are different bows for different situations.

Sealed with a Kiss

The air kiss is common in many regions, including Portugal, Latin America, Russia, the United Kingdom, and Ukraine, but usually among women or between men and women. Only in Argentina do men commonly air-kiss other men.

Kiss, Kiss

Depending on where you go in France, you may have to air-kiss up to four times on alternating cheeks to get your greeting across. In parts of Afghanistan, that number goes up to eight!

People in Thailand, India, Cambodia, and Laos greet each other by bowing slightly with their hands pressed together in a prayer position.

FIND YOUR TONGUE

Stick out your tongue to say hello in Tibet! Tibetan monks started this tradition to prove they weren't the reincarnation of a cruel, black-tongued king from the 9th century.

Just Breathe

On the Polynesian island of Tuvalu, it's traditional for people to press cheeks together and take a deep breath in welcome. In some parts of New Zealand, the Maori still practice the *hongi*, a greeting ritual involving touching noses and inhaling.

I Want Candy

Tootsie Rolls were named after their inventor Leo Hirschfield's daughter, whose nickname was Tootsie.

Special Delivery

Tootsie Rolls were used in rations for soldiers in World War I, but during the Korean War, American troops used the code "Tootsie Rolls" to mean ammunition. When the First Marine Division called for Tootsie Rolls at the battle of Chosin Reservoir, the radio operator didn't have the code sheet and made an airdrop of the chocolate candies!

M&M's are the most common form of chocolate sent with astronauts on flights to outer space.

EXTRATERRESTRIAL ADVERTISING

The Hershey Company paid Steven Spielberg $1 million to get Reese's Pieces featured in the blockbuster movie *E.T. the ExtraTerrestrial* as the lovable alien's favorite candy. Spielberg originally wanted to use M&M's, but the company turned down the offer!

STARBURSTS WERE INVENTED IN THE UNITED KINGDOM AND WERE ORIGINALLY CALLED OPAL FRUITS.

Cotton candy was originally called Fairy Floss, and one of its inventors was a dentist.

Mystery, Solved

The Dum Dums mystery flavor is sometimes a mix of two flavors. It happens when the candy-making machines switch to creating a new flavor.

BEAR-Y GUMMY

Which came first: the bear or the worm? **Gummy bears** were introduced **July 15, 1931**, and **gummy worms** came exactly **50 years** later.

The Sweet Spot

In 1905, Milton S. Hershey opened his chocolate company in Pennsylvania—but he didn't stop there. Hershey built a model town for his employees, known today as Hershey, Pennsylvania, complete with public transportation, an amusement park, and a public school system.

TRIPLE THREAT

The 3 Musketeers bar got its name from the ingredients. The early bars had three different kinds of nougat: vanilla, chocolate, and strawberry.

Snickers—the best-selling candy bar in the world—and the lollipop were both named after horses.

OPENING ACT

Before there were Reese's Cups, there were Lizzie Bars, chocolate-covered caramel and coconut, and Johnny Bars, candies made of molasses. Inventor (and former Hershey's employee!) Harry Burnett Reese debuted these candies named after his children before he struck gold with the Reese's Peanut Butter Cup.

Amazing Amusements

Slow and Steady

In 1884, the first roller-coaster-type ride in the United States debuted on Coney Island. At full speed, the Switchback Railway went a thrilling... 6 mph—but it only cost 5 cents to ride!

Zoom, Zoom

The **fastest** roller coaster in the world goes from **0 mph** to almost **150 mph** in only **4.9 seconds.** Located in Ferrari World, Abu Dhabi, this coaster—Formula Rossa—was built to evoke the speed and adrenaline of Formula One racing.

Pedal Pushers

The Sky Cycle roller coaster in Japan is more than 50 feet off the ground, and riders must pedal themselves in tandem-cycle cars. While it may not be a speedy ride, it can still get your adrenaline pumping: The track does not have a guard rail, so the only thing protecting riders from falling is a small seatbelt.

THE **MOST-VISITED** THEME PARK IN THE WORLD IS MAGIC KINGDOM IN **WALT DISNEY WORLD,** FLORIDA.

The King of Coasters

Both the fastest roller coaster in North America and the tallest roller coaster in the world are one and the same: Kingda Ka at Six Flags Great Adventure, New Jersey. The coaster drops riders from a height of 456 feet—about 45 stories high!

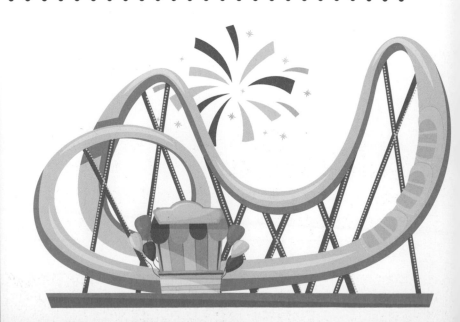

Word Search

Amusement Park Rides

Look at the puzzle below and see if you can find these names of amusement park rides. Circle the words going across, up and down, and diagonally. Some words may be backwards!

BUMPER CARS
CAROUSEL
FERRIS WHEEL
FUN HOUSE
GO-KARTS

HAUNTED HOUSE
LOG FLUME
PIRATE SHIP
ROLLER COASTER
SCRAMBLER

SLIDE
SWING RIDE
TEACUPS
TILT-A-WHIRL
ZIPPER

```
B S M S V S K N F N L U R C S
A F W K T J R U S R K O U A E
N E O I W R N A I F L V E R S
M D H T N H A H C L P S W O P
E I H D O G W K E R L X K U U
P L O U E A R R O R E C A S C
I S S A T L C I M G J P N E A
H E T L K O D E D W Y J M L E
S F I B A T D S Y E C N F U T
E T Y S C R A M B L E R O J B
T W T E S U O H D E T N U A H
A E Z I P P E R U I L W G U Y
R X X W U L E M U L F G O L I
I U V J Y Y K T O W M C U N U
P R L E E H W S I R R E F Z O
```

Gentle Giants

Gorillas have to build a new nest every single day because they never sleep in the same nest twice.

The biggest and oldest male in a troop is called the silverback because of the silver-colored strip of hair running down his back.

CUCKOO FOR KOKO

Koko, a gorilla raised in captivity, learned to communicate using American Sign Language (ASL). She knew more than 2,000 words, including "food," "sorry," and "flower." Koko used ASL to talk with her famous human friends, such as Robin Williams and Mr. Rogers.

K O K O

Koko's Kittens

Over the course of her life, Koko adopted and cared for two different kittens. She also named them both herself! The first she called All Ball, and the second she named Lips Lipstick.

Gorillas don't typically drink water—they get their hydration from the plants they eat.

When eating their favorite foods, gorillas often hum and sing—kind of like humans saying "mmm" when they're eating a delicious snack.

On average, gorillas weigh between **300** and **500 pounds**. That's about one-tenth as heavy as a car.

Because gorillas' arms are longer than their legs, they often do the "knuckle walk"—using the backs of their fingers like feet.

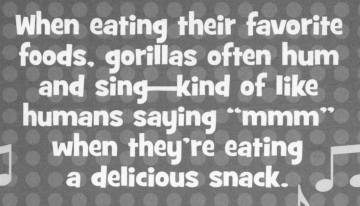

Hey There, Cousin!

Gorillas are one of the closest cousins to humans, sharing 98.3% of their genetic code. Gorillas can even show their emotions in similar ways to humans, such as laughing.

GORILLA FAMILIES, MADE UP OF UP TO **30 MEMBERS**, ARE CALLED **TROOPS**.

THE NOSE KNOWS

Like human fingerprints, researchers can use gorillas' nose prints to tell them apart. The depth and pattern of the wrinkles around the nose are totally unique to each gorilla.

165

Color My World

THE ORIGINAL EIGHT

THE FIRST BOX OF CRAYOLA CRAYONS WAS SOLD IN 1903 AND ONLY COST 5 CENTS. THE BOX HAD EIGHT COLORS:

RED, ORANGE, YELLOW, GREEN, BLUE, VIOLET, BLACK, AND BROWN.

THOSE ARE THE SAME COLORS YOU GET IN A BOX TODAY!

Wipe Away the Gripe

A chemist at Binney & Smith—the company that became Crayola—was out of new ideas, so he went to the complaint department and read the letters sent in by everyday folks. Many letters were from moms asking how to remove crayons from fabrics and walls, which inspired the chemist to create a washable crayon.

"LEFTOLAS" IS THE NAME FOR LEFTOVER CRAYONS THAT ARE TOO TINY TO USE.

By the age of 10, the average kid has worn down about 730 crayons.

THE POPULAR VOTE

In both 1993 and 2000, the Crayola Color Census conducted polls to find out the most popular colors in America. Blue topped the list both times.

Float On

Why do some crayons float, but others sink? Crayons are made of paraffin wax and pigment(s) that produce color, and each color requires a different amount of pigment. The crayons that require more pigment are denser, so they will sink.

HALL OF FAMERS

BETWEEN 1990 AND 2017, 13 DIFFERENT COLORS WERE RETIRED AND SENT TO THE CRAYOLA HALL OF FAME.

THOSE COLORS INCLUDED BLIZZARD BLUE, DANDELION, AND RAW UMBER.

The name Crayola, coined by Alice Binney, wife of the company's founder, comes from the French word for "chalk," craie, and the Latin root for "oily," ola.

COMMON SCENTS

According to a Yale University study, crayons are one of the top 20 most recognizable smells. What other items made the list? Lemons, peanut butter, and cat food.

Every year, Crayola makes almost 3 billion crayons, 600 million colored pencils, and 465 million markers.

There are 120 different colors of Crayola crayons, and many have silly, creative names such as:

PURPLE MOUNTAINS MAJESTY, MACARONI AND CHEESE, and JAZZBERRY JAM.

167

We Are the Champions

INTERNATIONAL MLB

Canada's Toronto Blue Jays are the only baseball team located outside of the United States to become World Series Champions. They won back-to-back in 1992 and 1993.

IN 1967, TICKETS TO THE FIRST SUPER BOWL COST ABOUT $12.

FOOTBALL

STATE CHAMPS

In 1935, the Detroit Tigers (MLB), Lions (NFL), and Red Wings (NHL) all won their first championships. At the time, the NBA had not yet been established, which means Detroit won all three major national professional sports championships in the same year!

EAST vs. WEST

Combined, the Los Angeles Lakers and the Boston Celtics have appeared in 34 of 71 NBA Finals championships. Of those, the rivals have played each other 12 times, with the Celtics winning nine of the 12 matchups.

TICKETS TO THE SUPER BOWL IN 2017 AVERAGED $4,744.

NOT SPELLING BEE CHAMPS

Since 1924, it's been an annual tradition to add the names of players on the winning team to the Stanley Cup. There are over 2,000 names engraved on the cup, with notable misspellings: Boston Bruins was once spelled "BQSTQN BRUINS" and the New York Islanders was once spelled "NEW YORK ILANDERS."

Black & Yellow

Pittsburgh, Pennsylvania, had a big year for sports in 2009. Their NFL team, the Steelers, won the Super Bowl, while their NHL team, the Penguins, won the Stanley Cup. As of 2018, that was the last time professional sports teams from the same city won their respective championships in the same year.

Trophy Time

The winning team of the Super Bowl is presented with the Vince Lombardi Trophy, named after the coach who led the Green Bay Packers to victory in the first and second Super Bowls. A new trophy is handmade by Tiffany & Co. jewelers each year and is estimated to take over four months to complete.

As of 2018, **only seven** baseball teams have **never won a World Series:** Colorado Rockies, Milwaukee Brewers, San Diego Padres, Seattle Mariners, Tampa Bay Rays, Texas Rangers, and Washington Nationals.

POOR SPORTS

In 1903, the first ever World Series went off without a hitch. The next year, the World Series, set to take place between the Boston Americans and the New York Giants, was canceled because of a dramatic personal feud between the team managers.

A PERFECT GAME

Pitching a perfect game, in which no batters reach base throughout all nine innings, is pretty difficult—only one pitcher at a World Series has ever done so! In the 1956 World Series between the New York Yankees and the Brooklyn Dodgers, Yankees pitcher Don Larsen threw a perfect game and led his team to a World Series victory.

I Spy Cool Facts

Buzz Off!

In the 1970s, the CIA created a listening device disguised as a dragonfly. This "bug-bug," called the Insectothopter, was a sleek, speedy, remote-controlled listening device. The only problem was that even the smallest gust of wind would throw the bug off course!

Secret Agent Woman

Agent 355 was an important member of the Culper spy ring, a group working for George Washington during the Revolutionary War. Later, Agent 355 was revealed to be a woman.

Cooking Up Secrets

Most people know Julia Child for her culinary skills, but during World War II she served her country by joining the Office of Strategic Services (now known as the CIA). Child handled highly classified documents and secret messages, and she even worked on developing a shark repellent to protect explosives targeting German U-boats.

Throughout history, spies have concealed secret cameras in many everyday objects: pens, buttons, key chains, briefcases, lighters, and even hairbrushes.

Espionage Education

Where do spies go to learn how to be spies? During World War II, British and American forces founded a facility, unofficially called Camp X, to teach the art of espionage. At Camp X, agents learned lock picking, intelligence gathering, encoding and decoding, and sabotage.

Treetop Troopers

During World War I, the French, British, and Germans would sneakily plant tall, iron trees along the front lines. Soldiers would climb up and into these observation trees, allowing them to closely spy on their enemies undetected.

A DISGUISE KIT ISSUED BY THE CIA IN THE 1960s CONTAINED GROOMING ITEMS, INCLUDING SCISSORS, TWEEZERS, AND A COMB, AS WELL AS A HEEL INSERT THAT COULD BE USED TO ALTER A PERSON'S WALK.

RESEARCH HAS SHOWN THAT SPIES ARE POTENTIALLY ABLE TO DETERMINE WHAT SOMEONE TYPES ON A KEYBOARD BASED SOLELY ON **SOUND.**

Birdbrained Heroism

Cher Ami was a carrier pigeon who served the US Army in France during World War I. While delivering his 12th secret message, he was shot through the body and legs but managed to drop off the message—carrying it on his wounded leg! For his bravery, he was awarded a French military honor.

CARD-TOGRAPHY ♣ ♦ ♠ ♥

During the second World War, the US government teamed up with a playing-card company to create a deck with maps fixed together in between the layers of paper that make up a card. The maps' detailed routes intended to aid Allied prisoners in their escape—and the card deck is still kept secret today!

Throughout history, many animals have been accused of being used as spies: SHARKS, MONKEYS, PIGEONS, DOLPHINS, CATS, DOGS, VULTURES, and even SQUIRRELS!

You Ate...What?

Foods from Around the World

HOW LARVA-LY

With a name that means "rotting cheese," *casu marzu* gets its sharp taste from the maggots that have hatched and lived inside it. This Sardinian dairy delight can be served with or without its maggots—but be careful! They can jump into your eyes if you decide to eat them.

I SCREAM FOR...

You won't find this in the freezer section! From the Yupik word meaning "mix them together," and nicknamed "Eskimo ice cream," *akutaq* is a unique blend of whipped animal fat and oil with berries that varies in recipe from family to family in Alaska and Canada.

NOT EGGS-ACTLY WHAT YOU THINK

Century eggs are not really that old. This Chinese delicacy consists of duck, chicken, or quail eggs preserved for a few weeks or months. The preservation process turns the egg whites black, makes their yolks green and creamy, and gives them a strong odor.

Don't Put This in SPAM

Although sometimes called "mystery meat," SPAM is made of canned pork shoulder, ham, salt, water, sugar, potato starch, and sodium nitrate. The real mystery is what its name means; only a few top executives at Hormel, the US-based company that makes SPAM, know the truth.

FAIRY WEIRD

There's nothing magical about fairy bread: It's just a piece of white bread with butter spread on top and covered with rainbow sprinkles! Even so, it's a nostalgic favorite in Australia usually made for kids.

Talk About Pigging Out

Guinea pigs in various Andean countries are not typically seen as pets; instead, they're called *cuy* and considered a delicacy. In fact, there are actual cuy farms that raise these animals like livestock.

WHAT'S THAT SMELL?

Why, it's *surströmming*, a northern Swedish dish made of Baltic Sea herring that's fermented in salt and usually sold in cans. It smells like rotten eggs, and the scent is so strong that it often needs to be eaten outside!

SURSTRÖMMING

That's No Mushroom

Huitlacoche, otherwise known as corn smut, is a plant disease that grows like tumors on rotting corn kernels. This gray, spreadable fungus has a woody flavor, is very nutritious, and can be used in a variety of Mexican dishes— even quesadillas!

173

Mellow Yellow

The word "banana" is said to derive from the Arabic word banan, meaning "finger."

BANANAS are one of the most popular fruits, with around 114 MILLION METRIC TONS eaten worldwide each year—about the same weight as 19 ELEPHANTS!

LEMONY COMBO

One common type of lemon, native to China, is called the Meyer lemon. It's actually a combination of a lemon and a mandarin orange!

The Midas Touch

In 2014, scientists discovered a new species of bat in South America. Because of the animal's golden-yellow fur, the bat was named *Myotis midastactus* after the story of King Midas and his golden touch.

GOLDFINCHES MAKE A COMMON CALL WHEN FLYING THAT SOUNDS LIKE THEY'RE SAYING "POTATO CHIP."

She Works Hard for the Honey

It takes the nectar from **2 million** flowers to make a **single pound** of honey. On **one collection trip**, a bee visits anywhere from **50 to 100 flowers.**

OF ALL INSECTS, BEES ARE THE ONLY ONES THAT PRODUCE FOOD EATEN BY HUMANS.

When Life Hands You Lemons

Make Invisible Ink

Lemon juice has been used throughout history as a way to write hidden messages. Spies could hide their secrets in plain sight with this invisible ink—and you can, too!

Make your own invisible ink, using these materials:

½ lemon (OR 1 tablespoon lemon juice)   bowl   cotton swabs   white paper   lamp or other light source

DIRECTIONS

1. Squeeze ½ lemon into the bowl. Using bottled lemon juice works just fine as well; about 1 tablespoon is a good amount to start with.

2. Dip the cotton swab into the liquid and write or draw on the paper.

3. Let dry fully.

4. Once dry, hold the paper over a warm lamp, being careful not to touch the bulb.

What happens to your message?

This and That

Q The letter *Q* is the only letter that does not appear in the name of any US state.

Cats only sweat through their paws.

Big Bird is 8'2"—more than a foot taller than basketball great Shaquille O'Neal, who is 7'1".

Disney princesses who marry into royalty (Cinderella, Belle, and Tiana) wear gloves, while princesses born royal do not.

THE FIRST ONE-CENT COIN IN THE UNITED STATES WAS SUPPOSEDLY DESIGNED BY BEN FRANKLIN AND CONTAINED THE PHRASE "MIND YOUR BUSINESS."

SWEET SCIENCE

Engineering students from Purdue University created a machine modeled after a human tongue to try to determine HOW MANY LICKS it takes to get to the CENTER of a TOOTSIE ROLL POP. It took the MACHINE an average of 364 LICKS, but when they replicated the experiment with HUMANS it took them an average of 252 LICKS.

According to researchers, over 72% of people feel it's okay to eat pizza for both breakfast and dinner on the same day.

The **King of Hearts** is the **only** one of the four kings in a deck of cards that does **not** have a **mustache.**

Handle with Care

It's been more than 100 years since Marie Curie conducted her research, but her journals and notes are still radioactive! Modern-day scientists interested in seeing the items, located at the National Library in Paris, have to sign a safety waiver and wear protective clothing.

ON AVERAGE, AN AMERICAN SPENDS ABOUT **$1,100 A YEAR ON COFFEE.**

WHITE CHOCOLATE ISN'T TECHNICALLY CHOCOLATE BECAUSE IT DOESN'T CONTAIN ANY COCOA SOLIDS.

The ancient Aztecs used cocoa beans as currency—the better the quality, the more the bean was worth.

Up, Up, and Away

UP WHERE THE AIR IS CLEAR

The earliest kite flying dates back to around 200 BC, used by Chinese General Han Hsin of the Han Dynasty. Planning to attack a walled-off city, Hsin flew a kite over the wall and used the length of the string to measure the distance needed to tunnel under the wall. His measurements were correct, and his troops surprised and defeated the enemy.

★ HIGH-FLYING HOMEWORK ★

The current United States flag was designed in 1958 by a 17-year-old high-school student who created it for a school project and submitted the design to a national contest. Among the 1,500 submissions, his was selected by President Eisenhower to become the official flag. His original grade on the homework assignment? B-.

Nepal is the only country with a national flag that is not a rectangle; it is two pennant shapes united on top of each other.

CATCH THIS

Local kids in New Haven, Connecticut, played a game in which they tossed empty pie plates from the Frisbie Pie Company and called out, "Frisbie," which eventually gained popularity at nearby Yale University. When West Coast toy company Wham-O developed a similar plastic toy and heard about the popularity of the East Coast Frisbie, they changed the name of their toy to Frisbee®.

Don't Look Down!

The highest recorded flight by a hot-air balloon reached 68,986 feet over Mumbai, India. The average jet aircraft typically cruises somewhere between 31,000 and 38,000 feet.

The hot-air balloon is the oldest flight technology that successfully carries humans.

Weather Rules

Hot-air balloons cannot fly in the rain. The balloons get quite hot, but the rain falling on them creates temperatures too cool to be successfully manned.

Barnyard Ballooners

In the late 1700s, brothers Joseph and Etienne Montgolfier experimented with designs for their hot-air balloon concept. To test their invention, they sent the balloon up with some animal passengers: a duck, a rooster, and a sheep.

FLIGHT FRIGHT

Aerophobia is the **fear** of flying. This fear affects about **6.5% of Americans**—approximately **20 million people!**

De-fact-cation: Fun Facts About Poop

You Look Poo-tiful

Ancient Romans mixed crocodile feces into their mud baths and face masks. They also used pigeon poop to dye their hair blonde.

Poop is actually 75% water.

POO GOES THERE?

The word "poop" originates from the Middle English word poupen or popen, which means "to fart."

FART!

ARE YOU FECE-ING THIS?

The Laetoli footprints, one of the most important fossils ever found, were discovered accidentally during an elephant-dung fight between two paleoanthropologists.

WHAT A WASTE!

Did you know that your **poop** contains traces of precious metals like **gold** and **silver**? The waste produced by **1 million** Americans may be worth as much as **$13 million**.

(POOP) CHUTE FOR THE MOON

If you see a shooting star at night, it may just be a burning bag of astronaut poop ejected from a space station. There are also 96 bags of puke, pee, and poop that astronauts from the Apollo mission left behind on the moon.

YOU DUNG READING?

If you experience the Mariko Aoki phenomenon, you may feel a strong need to poop upon entering a bookstore.

Something Smells...Fishy

When parrotfish digest coral, they poop it out as sand. Because of this, a number of famous white sand beaches in Hawaii, the Maldives, and the Caribbean are partially made of fish poop.

Pet Pals

GOLDFISH
do not have stomachs.

PAWS PREFERRED
Cats are right- or left-handed. Researchers have found that male cats often favor their left paws while female cats prefer their right paws.

PRICEY PETS
HORSES are excellent animals, but on average, a horse costs **$2,500 TO $3,600** annually to keep as a pet. A pet **CAT OR DOG** typically costs **$500 TO $1,200** a year.

A HAMSTER'S TEETH NEVER STOP GROWING.

A group of **KITTENS** is called a **KINDLE**, and a group of **CATS** is called a **CLOWDER**.

Feathered Friends Forever

The most popular bird breeds to keep as pets are cockatiels, African grey parrots, parakeets, and macaws. A pet macaw is quite a long-term commitment, as these birds often live to be 50 years old.

Cats often dream while they sleep—just like humans.

Cats cannot taste sweet flavors, unlike most other mammals.

The name "ferret" comes from a Latin word for "little thief."

LUCK OF THE FELINE

Ancient Egyptians worshiped cats, as they believed the animals possessed magical powers and good luck. If a pet cat died, its owner would shave off his or her own eyebrows as a sign of mourning. If someone killed a cat, even by accident, he or she was met with harsh punishment—a death sentence.

Scent Sense

Hamsters have bad eyesight and rely on their sense of smell to navigate the world around them. They rub the scent glands on their backs on objects in order to leave a trail they can smell to find their way back.

In the 1100s, only Chinese royalty were allowed to have yellow goldfish in their homes because yellow was the official color of the emperor.

The whiskers on a cat's face are as sensitive as human fingertips.

The Curious States of America

According to researchers, Hawaii is the happiest state in America, followed by Utah and Minnesota.

One and Only in Monowi

Monowi, Nebraska, has a population of one. The village's only citizen, Elsie, serves as the town's mayor, bartender, and librarian.

1

LOST LOOT

Scottsboro, Alabama, is home to the Unclaimed Baggage Center, where you can purchase items found in lost airline luggage. Among the items found: a Dora the Explorer piñata, $10,000 engagement rings, a painting made by an elephant, antique wooden snowshoes, and a live rattlesnake!

In 2017, the amount of money casinos on the LAS VEGAS strip EARNED from gamblers totaled a hefty $6.5 BILLION—that's a lot of losses!

Make Way for Squirrels

The town of Longview, Washington, built a bridge over a busy roadway so that squirrels could cross over safely. The bridge, built in 1963, is named the Nutty Narrows Bridge.

One Cool Deal

Russia sold Alaska to the United States back in 1867. It cost $7.2 million, which works out to be only 2 cents an acre.

In 1893, a constitutional amendment was proposed to rename the United States as the "United States of the Earth."

Denver International Airport in Colorado is the largest airport in the United States and is twice the size of Manhattan.

In the United States, one out of every 38 people lives in New York City.

There are about 107,651 miles of rivers in the state of Idaho, which measures about half the distance from Earth to the moon.

Hawaii and Arizona are the only states that do not follow daylight saving time.

KANSAS PRODUCES ENOUGH WHEAT EVERY YEAR TO FEED THE ENTIRE WORLD POPULATION FOR ABOUT TWO WEEKS.

Corn You Believe It?

CANDY CORN IS DESIGNED TO LOOK LIKE AN EAR OF CORN WHEN THE PIECES ARE STACKED TOGETHER.

Popular Popcorn

Every year, Americans consume an average of 13 billion quarts of popped popcorn. That's about 42 quarts per person!

CORN OR CORN PRODUCTS CAN BE FOUND IN BATTERIES, CRAYONS, AND FIREWORKS.

Corn is grown on every continent in the world except Antarctica.

Golden State

The United States grows a lot of corn—about 97 million acres worth. That's about the size of the state of California!

Corny Celebrations

You can celebrate corn, also known as maize, during a few national holidays: National Popcorn Day is January 19; National Corn on the Cob Day is June 11; and National Candy Corn Day is October 30.

ONE EAR OF CORN HAS AN AVERAGE OF 800 KERNELS.

Maize Maze
Lending an Ear

One of the largest corn mazes can be found at Cool Patch Pumpkins in Dixon, California. It's easy to get lost in the maze's 60 acres of corn.

Follow the maze to see if you can navigate up, down, and around the kernels in the ear of corn below to get from one end to the other!

START

FINISH

Answers on page 308

The Puck Stops Here

THE ANAHEIM DUCKS ARE NAMED AFTER THE DISNEY MOVIE **THE MIGHTY DUCKS.**

DURING A HOCKEY GAME, IF ALL THE TEAM GOALIES ARE INJURED, ANYONE INSIDE THE ARENA CAN SUIT UP TO PLAY.

THE FIRST INDOOR HOCKEY GAME WAS PLAYED IN MONTREAL IN 1875, WHEN ORGANIZER JAMES CREIGHTON CAME UP WITH THE FIRST SET OF RULES, ALONG WITH THE VERY FIRST PUCK—MADE OF WOOD!

Each **PLAYER** on the championship team gets to keep the **STANLEY CUP** for **A DAY**, so it's been **LOST**, tossed in **POOLS**, and used to hold anything from **CEREAL** and **POPCORN** to **DOG FOOD** and **BABIES!**

STICK SHIFT

Before the 1960s, hockey sticks were stick-straight. Chicago Blackhawk Stan Mikita accidentally cracked his stick so it bent during practice. He kept playing—and the curved stick was born!

Hockey History

THE STANLEY CUP TROPHY IS OLDER THAN THE NATIONAL HOCKEY LEAGUE (NHL)! CANADA'S LORD ARTHUR STANLEY DONATED THE CUP FOR AMATEUR HOCKEY CHAMPIONSHIPS IN 1892, AND THE LEAGUE WAS FORMED IN 1917.

Pittsburgh Penguin star Sidney Crosby is the youngest NHL player to reach 100 points in a season, the youngest to win a scoring title, and the youngest to be named captain—all by the time he was 19 years old.

In the late 1960s, the Pittsburgh Penguins had a live mascot, a penguin named Slapshot Pete.

Goalie Girl

Manon Rheaume was the first woman to play in the NHL. On September 24, 1992, the 20-year-old tended goal for one period in an exhibition game as a member of the Tampa Bay Lightning.

© Jerry Coli | Dreamstime.com

Wayne "The Great One" Gretzky holds the record for breaking the most records—more than 60!

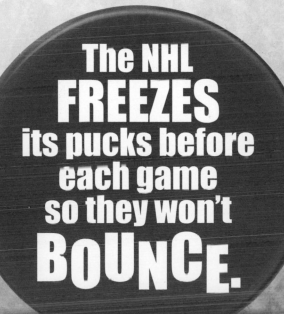

The NHL **FREEZES** its pucks before each game so they won't **BOUNCE.**

"Weight"-ing for the Win

The **March 25, 1936,** matchup between the Detroit Red Wings and the Montreal Maroons—the **longest game in history**—didn't end until **2:25 a.m.,** after **116 minutes and 30 seconds** of overtime. The **winning goalie,** Red Wing Normie Smith, reportedly **lost 12 pounds** while he stopped **92 shots!**

Right on the Money

THE FIRST FIRST LADY

Martha Washington was the first—and only—First Lady of the United States to be pictured on paper money. The $1 silver certificate was issued in 1886, six years after George was placed on the dollar bill.

A DIME HAS 118 RIDGES ON IT.

If you had $10 BILLION in $1 BILLS and spent $1 EVERY SECOND, it would take 317 YEARS to SPEND it all!

Of all the bills produced by the US Bureau of Engraving and Printing, about 45% are $1 bills.

TIME FOR A CHANGE

Care to make change for a dollar? You have plenty of options: There are 293 ways to do so!

Paper money isn't made out of paper at all; it's fabric.

CRITTER CURRENCY

Along with some of the country's famous human residents, Australian currency also includes images of national critters: The $1 coin has a picture of five kangaroos, the 10-cent coin shows a male lyrebird dancing, and the 5-cent coin depicts an echidna.

Australians

refer to $20 bills as **lobsters** because of their red color, and they call their yellow $50 bills **pineapples.**

The time listed on the clock on the back of a $100 bill is 4:10—and there's no record of why that time was chosen.

IF YOU WERE TO FOLD A US BILL OVER AND OVER, IT WOULD TAKE ABOUT 4,000 FOLDS FORWARD AND BACKWARD UNTIL THE BILL WOULD TEAR.

THE WORLD'S OLDEST CURRENCY STILL IN USE IS THE POUND STERLING, ORIGINATING IN ENGLAND 1,200 YEARS AGO.

To prevent fraud, the image-editing program Adobe Photoshop can detect when a protected image of currency is opened, and the program shuts down.

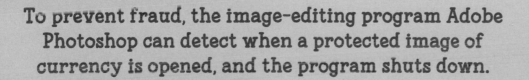

Ps

Planes, Trains, and Automobiles

One of the world's fastest trains is the Shanghai Maglev, which takes a seven-minute journey about 19 miles from the city center to the airport at a speedy 267 miles per hour.

AROUND 75% OF ALL THE ROLLS-ROYCES EVER MADE ARE STILL ON THE ROAD.

POWERED BY HORSE

James Watt coined the term "horsepower" as a marketing tool while designing a steam engine in the 1760s. He calculated how much power one horse could yield over a specific amount of time, as well as the amount of power his steam engine could generate. Explaining it as horsepower, Watt let people know how much money they would save by how many horses they would be able to replace.

WHITE, SILVER, AND BLACK ARE THE MOST POPULAR CAR COLORS—ABOUT 50% OF ALL CARS ON THE ROAD ARE ONE OF THESE SHADES.

English became the official language used by international pilots and controllers in 2008, when the International Civil Aviation Organization required all members from the 185 countries to pass an English test in order to improve safety and prevent communication errors.

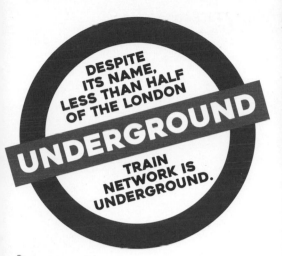

UNDERGROUND

DESPITE ITS NAME, LESS THAN HALF OF THE LONDON

TRAIN NETWORK IS UNDERGROUND.

The average US commercial airplane is struck by lightning at least once a year, which might sound scary, but airplanes are rigorously designed and tested to protect against damage from strikes.

It is estimated that less than 20% of the world's population has ever taken a flight.

Worldwide, only about one-third of countries drive on the left side of the road.

AT ANY GIVEN TIME, THERE ARE AN AVERAGE OF 5,000 COMMERCIAL AIRPLANES FLYING OVER THE UNITED STATES.

THE AVERAGE CAR HAS AROUND 30,000 INDIVIDUAL PARTS.

THERE ARE CURRENTLY ABOUT 1 BILLION CARS IN USE THROUGHOUT THE WORLD.

I, O, U, AND SOMETIMES Y

The letters *I*, *O*, *U*, and *Y* are the only letters of the alphabet that have never been used at any time in the New York City subway system. Letters *I* and *O* are too similar to numbers 1 and 0, while *U* and *Y* are avoided because of any potential confusion between them and "you" and "why."

Crazy Collections

BIG and Tiny

Erika Nelson is the creator of the World's Largest Collection of the World's Smallest Versions of the World's Largest Things, a collection of small versions of landmarks, items, and places that hold the title of "world's largest." The collection includes items such as tiny versions of water towers, a ball of twine, and a Paul Bunyan statue.

The owner of the largest collection of Superman memorabilia, with over 1,500 items, is such a big fan that he legally changed his middle name to **SUPERMAN!**

The Burger King

A collection owned by a man known as Hamburger Harry is filled with 3,724 hamburger-related items. There are Happy Meal toys, stuffed toy hamburgers, posters, and clothing, along with unexpected items like a custom-built hamburger motorcycle and a $3,500 hamburger bed.

In **Arizona**, a collection of over **8,600 bottles** of **hot sauce** includes some wild finds: a container shaped like **a sword**, a gold-covered **skull**, and one made with **edible black ants**.

BOUNTIFUL BEARS

A South Dakota woman's tremendous collection of teddy bears contains over 8,000 different bears. The tiniest bear in the collection is just ¾ inches tall, while the tallest is almost 8 feet.

A Gift of a Globe

The American Geographic Society in Wisconsin holds a collection of 520,000 maps, including more than 220 unique globes. One of the heaviest and most notable is the President's Globe, weighing over 750 pounds. This rare globe was made for President Roosevelt during World War II, and a matching one was gifted to British Prime Minister Winston Churchill.

The two-time record holder for the largest snow globe collection now owns 4,059 snow globes—including 439 Christmas-themed ones.

Boasting a whopping 19,571 individual items, a German woman's record-holding collection of erasers includes items from 112 different countries.

A PENNY SAVED

In 2005, an Alabama man cashed in his collection of pennies at a local bank. He had **1,308,459 pennies**, worth **$13,084.59**. The collection weighed over **4½ tons**, which is almost as much as a hippopotamus!

KOOKY FOR COOKIE JARS

Grannie's Cookie Jars & Ice Cream Parlor in Indiana is home to a record-holding 2,653 cookie jars. Visitors can purchase any of the jars, as well as something from the parlor's collection of more than 1,000 salt-and-pepper shakers.

COOKIE

Get to Class!

Of all the letters in the English alphabet, the letter **E** is used most often.

Pencils were first mass-produced in Germany in 1662.

Lady in Waiting

The *Mona Lisa* may have taken 16 years to complete. Leonardo da Vinci started the painting in 1503, and it was found in his studio after his death in 1519.

Kickball, invented around 1917 in Ohio, was originally played with a soccer ball and called Kick Baseball.

Every Word Counts

There are only 50 different words used in the entirety of *Green Eggs and Ham*. Why? Dr. Seuss's editor bet that he couldn't write a book using fewer words than the 225 used in *The Cat in the Hat*.

The first tennis courts were hourglass-shaped.

$$111{,}111{,}111 \times 111{,}111{,}111 =$$

Around 1 million Earths could fit inside the sun.

The word "independence" does not appear in the Declaration of Independence.

The Word Turned Upside Down

Ambigrams are words or symbols that look the same from different perspectives (upside down, right to left, etc.). One example is the word "SWIMS."

SWIMS

A Number to Remember

The world record holder for memorizing the most numerals of pi knew a staggering **70,000 decimal places.** The process took **10 hours** to recite—all while blindfolded.

J is the only letter not found on the periodic table.

Pi written out backward to two decimal places spells "PIE":
π

A SECOND IS CALLED A SECOND BECAUSE IT IS THE SECOND DIVISION OF AN HOUR AFTER A MINUTE.

12,345,678,987,654,321

TV Guide

Doctor's Orders

Doctor Who is the longest-running science fiction TV series of all time. It ran from 1963 to 1989, returning in 2005, and 13 actors have played the title character. In 2018, Jodi Whitaker became the first female actor to be given the role of the time-traveling Doctor.

The first television commercial ever aired in 1941, advertising Bulova watches—and it cost the company $9.

Field Work

A 14-year-old farm boy named Philo Farnsworth came up with the idea for electronic television while plowing a field. He demonstrated the first working all-electronic television in 1927, at age 21, and received over 300 patents related to television and other devices throughout his lifetime.

FROM 1949 TO 1950, AMERICANS WATCHED OVER **FOUR HOURS** OF TELEVISION PER DAY, AND THAT NUMBER WENT UP TO NEARLY **EIGHT HOURS** IN 2018 FOR THE AVERAGE AMERICAN HOUSEHOLD.

Color TV sets weren't common across the United States until the 1970s.

POLICE PUBLIC CALL BOX

POLICE TELEPHONE
FREE
FOR USE OF
PUBLIC

ADVICE & ASSISTANCE
OBTAINABLE IMMEDIATELY

OFFICER & CARS
RESPOND TO ALL CALLS

PULL TO OPEN

ABOUT 1% OF THE STATIC IN AN ANALOG TELEVISION IS MADE UP OF LEFTOVER ENERGY FROM THE BIG BANG, CALLED THE COSMIC MICROWAVE BACKGROUND.

Studies show that our brains have a hard time distinguishing fictional characters from real people, so our relationships to TV characters feel personal.

Despite inventing the first working electronic television, Philo Farnsworth didn't think there was anything worthwhile on TV and didn't want his family to watch it.

Mouse, Interrupted

The BBC shut down for almost seven years during World War II. On September 1, 1939, two days before Britain declared war on Germany, the BBC went off the air right after a Mickey Mouse cartoon. When the network returned after the war in 1946, broadcasting resumed with the very same cartoon.

The longest-running program in the history of television is the American show Meet the Press, which debuted in 1947.

NOVEMBER

21

is World Television Day.

In 1909, **decades before** the **first TV** set was up and running, Russian scientist **Constantin Perskyi** introduced the word **"television"** during the first International Congress of Electricity in Paris.

German inventor Paul Nipkow created his "electric telescope," which produced a static black-and-white transmission, in 1884, before the word "television" even existed.

Building Blocks

OUCH!

It hurts to step on a LEGO® brick, because it can withstand 950 pounds before it cracks—that's about as heavy as a grand piano.

Using six 2x4 LEGO® bricks of the same color, you could make more than 915 million possible combinations.

There are about 65 LEGO® bricks for each of the Earth's 6 billion inhabitants.

The word "lego" is a combination of Danish words *leg* and *godt*, which together mean "play well."

If you made a line of all the LEGO® bricks sold in just one year, it would be long enough to circle the world five times.

SINCE 1949—THE YEAR THE FIRST VERSION OF AUTOMATIC BINDING BRICKS (THE EARLY NAME FOR THE LEGO®) WERE PRODUCED—THERE HAVE BEEN 400 BILLION LEGO® BRICKS MADE.

There are little numbers printed on the inside of every LEGO® brick, which refer to the specific mold used at the factory.

Around **36,000** LEGO® pieces are made every minute, **24** hours a day, **7** days a week— about **19 billion** LEGO® pieces a year!

Spot the Difference
Toy House

Find and circle 10 differences between these two pictures of a LEGO® house.

Answers on page 309

This and That

IN 1916, JEANNETTE RANKIN WAS THE FIRST WOMAN ELECTED TO THE US CONGRESS— FOUR YEARS BEFORE THE 19TH AMENDMENT GRANTED WOMEN THE RIGHT TO VOTE.

THE **ENTIRE** STATE OF **WYOMING** ONLY HAS **TWO ESCALATORS**.

The average cloud weighs about 1 million pounds.

The POPULATION of New York City is GREATER than that of 40 US STATES.

Central Park in New York City cost just about as much as the state of Alaska.

The ABCs of 123

If you were to write out every number ("one," "two," "three," etc.), you wouldn't use the letter *A* until you reached "one thousand." You wouldn't use the letter *B* until you reached "one billion."

Watermelon can be classified as both a fruit and a vegetable.

Part of the filling in between the wafers in a Kit Kat is made of other, rejected Kit Kats mashed together.

SHUFFLE AND REPEAT

In a standard 52-card deck, there are almost an infinite number of ways to arrange the order of the deck. This means that every time you shuffle a deck, you are almost certainly creating a unique arrangement of cards.

ROUGHLY 27,000 TREES WORTH OF TOILET PAPER IS USED DAILY WORLDWIDE.

Red Sour Patch Kids and Swedish Fish are the same candy with the exception of sour sugar.

The Scottish people have 421 words for snow!

TONKA TRUCKS GET THEIR NAME FROM LAKE MINNETONKA.

Park It!

Many visitors have reported seeing UFOs and strange, flashing lights at Colorado's Great Sand Dunes National Park.

PUP ENFORCEMENT

Glacier National Park in Montana has a "bark ranger," a border collie named Gracie, who works with human park rangers to help protect visitors from the park's wildlife. Among her duties, Gracie is in charge of herding goats, sheep, and other animals away from visitors' trails.

Cursed Souvenirs

Legend has it that visitors who take lava rocks from Hawaii's Volcanoes National Park will be cursed by Pele, a volcano goddess. The National Parks Service (NPS) disputes the legend, but that hasn't stopped hundreds of visitors from mailing their stolen rocks back to the NPS.

Not The Good Lands

Badlands National Park gets its name from its rugged, rocky terrain. When the Lakota Native Americans moved to that area of South Dakota, they referred to it as *mako sica*, translated as "land bad," and French visitors referred to it as *les mauvaises terres a traverser*, roughly translated as "bad lands to traverse."

Across America, more than 85 million acres of land are a part of the National Park System—almost the same size as the entire state of Montana.

Yellowstone National Park is America's first national park, established in 1872 by President Ulysses S. Grant.

← YELLOWSTONE NAT'L PARK

ROY SULLIVAN, a longtime park ranger at **SHENANDOAH NATIONAL PARK** in Virginia, holds the distinction of **SURVIVING** the most **LIGHTNING** strikes: **SEVEN TIMES!**

Smoky Mountains National Park is also known as the "Salamander Capital of the World" because of the more than 30 unique types of salamanders that reside there.

ROYAL-TREE

The General Sherman Tree is a sequoia found at Sequoia National Park in California. This "King of the Forest" is an estimated 2,100 years old and weighs 2.7 million pounds.

The Last Frontier

Wrangell St. Elias in Alaska is the largest national park in the United States. Spanning 13.2 million acres, the park is larger than Yosemite, Yellowstone, and the entire country of Switzerland combined.

Way Down Below

Crater Lake National Park in Oregon is home to the country's deepest lake, reaching depths of 1,949 feet. If you placed Chicago's Willis Tower, one of the world's tallest buildings, at the bottom of the lake, there would still be almost 500 feet needed to reach the surface.

Check Out These Facts

With a **book** checked out in **April 1955** and **returned 47 years later,** an Illinois woman holds a record for one of the **largest** overdue library book **fines**— **totaling $345.14.**

Worth a Read

Founded by Ben Franklin and his friends in the 1700s, the Library Company was the first subscription lending library in the United States. Books were expensive and hard to obtain, so the library—which required a membership fee— allowed locals to read hard-to-access materials.

The iconic LION STATUES perched outside the main branch of the NEW YORK PUBLIC LIBRARY are named PATIENCE and FORTITUDE.

GOING TO THE DOGS

In 2011, the law school library at Yale University had a furry friend that could be borrowed—a terrier named Monty. Monty has since retired from his career as a therapy dog, and new pups are being trained in his place.

Books by the Mile

The Library of Congress contains about 838 miles of bookshelves. That's about three times as long as the Grand Canyon! The smallest book in the library measures $1/25$ square inch—about the size of a period mark— and the biggest book measures 5 feet by 7 feet.

FANGS A LOT

Guests at the Joanina Library in Portugal are used to seeing bats swooping between the shelves. These high-flying residents serve an important purpose: eating insects in the library that could damage the books.

There are an estimated 116,867 libraries in the United States, and the average American checks out eight books a year.

LIBRARIANS HAVE FOUND SOME ODD ITEMS IN RETURNED BOOKS THAT PEOPLE USED AS BOOKMARKS: LEAVES, FLOWERS, MONEY, LOVE LETTERS, DIVORCE PAPERS, KNIVES, AND EVEN SLICES OF BACON.

Many public libraries now offer seed libraries, which allow people to "check out" different types of seeds to plant in their gardens or lend seeds to other members of the community.

BOOKS

China is home to many self-service libraries: vending machines located on public streets where patrons can choose among hundreds of books to check out on the spot.

THE LIBRARY BOOK **MOST OFTEN STOLEN** IS THE *GUINNESS BOOK OF WORLD RECORDS.*

It's a Bird! It's a Plane! It's Comic Book Facts!

Wakanda Wealth

Black Panther is the richest superhero; he's worth a staggering $90 trillion! By comparison, Iron Man, the second richest superhero, is only worth billions.

TO TELL THE TRUTH

The creator of Wonder Woman, William Moulton Marston, invented an early version of the lie detector test. That may explain why Wonder Woman's weapon is the Lasso of Truth!

MARVEL'S SPIDER-MAN HAS A HYPHEN BECAUSE STAN LEE WORRIED THAT READERS WOULD CONFUSE THE HERO WITH DC'S SUPERMAN.

© Starstock | Dreamstime.com

Iconic superhero creator Stan Lee was best known for creating the Avengers, Spider-Man, and the X-Men, but he created over 340 different heroes and villains over the course of his career.

JOLLY GRAY GIANT

The Incredible Hulk was originally designed as gray, but the printing press had trouble maintaining the same shade throughout the first issue. The creators decided to go with green instead.

LONGTIME FAN

A California man's record-holding COLLECTION of COMIC BOOKS contains 101,822 unique items. He's been collecting since he was a child and READS over 100 new comic books EVERY MONTH.

A Super Debut

Superman's first ever appearance was in *Action Comics No. 1*, published in 1938. The original price was 10 cents, but in 2014 a copy of the issue sold for over $3.2 million.

WHILE MANY THINK IT'S IN NEW YORK, GOTHAM CITY IS MORE LIKELY LOCATED IN NEW JERSEY.

The word "brainiac" as we know it likely originated from a supervillain of the same name in the Superman comics.

ON REPEAT

"DC" stands for "Detective Comics" after the publisher's popular 1930s crime series. Nowadays when we commonly refer to "DC Comics," it's redundant.

The Library of Congress is home to the world's largest public collection of comic books—over 140,000 items.

Of the multiverses in Marvel Comics, Earth-1218 is the version that is our reality.

Dig Up These Facts

The distance between footprints in a trackway can be used to estimate a dinosaur's speed.

TIMING IS EVERYTHING

Not all dinosaur species lived at the same time. For example, the *Stegosaurus* lived about 150 million years ago while the *Tyrannosaurus rex* lived about 72 million years ago—meaning the two dinosaurs walked the Earth millions of years apart.

Following in Their Footsteps

Dinosaur State Park in Connecticut is home to one of the largest dinosaur track sites in North America. There you can follow the trackways, a series of fossilized footprints, made by dinosaurs over 200 million years ago.

A BIG BITE

Scientists estimate that the *Allosaurus* was able to open its gigantic jaws between 79 and 92 degrees, which allowed it to capture large prey. That's wider than the jaw of a *Tyrannosaurus rex*!

JURASSIC TERMINAL

A fast-paced, modern place like an airport seems like the last place you would see a dinosaur, but at Chicago's O'Hare International Airport, you can do just that! Located in Terminal 1 is a towering 75-foot-long skeletal replica of a *Brachiosaurus*.

Plenty of animals we're familiar with today—such as sharks, cockroaches, bees, crocodiles, and the duck-billed platypus—were around when dinosaurs roamed the planet.

TOP (AND BOTTOM) OF THE CLASS

The size of the brain in relation to the size of the body is how scientists estimate a dinosaur's intelligence. One of the smartest dinosaurs was likely the *Troodon*, a tiny, birdlike dinosaur that had a brain proportionally larger than its slender size. The *Stegosaurus* had proportionally the smallest brain—the size of a walnut!

THE *MICRORAPTOR* WAS NAMED FOR ITS TINY SIZE; IT WEIGHED LESS THAN A POUND.

Scientists have discovered and named around **700 DIFFERENT TYPES** of dinosaurs.

DINOSAUR FOSSILS HAVE BEEN FOUND ON EVERY CONTINENT, EVEN ANTARCTICA.

By Any Other Name

Dinosaurs were generally named after where they lived, what they looked like, or who discovered them. Typically, Greek and Latin words were used: For example, *Stegosaurus* is a combination of the Greek *stegos*, or "roof," and *sauros*, meaning "lizard."

Women Take the Court

SHE CALLS THE SHOTS

The WNBA ball is 1 inch smaller than the NBA ball. The quarters are 10 minutes, two minutes shorter than NBA quarters. As for the shot clock, it was originally set at 30 seconds but now matches the NBA time at 24.

SHE WAS A SHOE-IN

In 1995, for only the second time in history, Nike named a sneaker after a basketball star. The player: WNBA standout Sheryl Swoopes. The shoe: Air Swoopes.

From 1936 to 1986, the All American Red Heads—with every player sporting bright red hair—toured the United States playing men's teams, winning the majority of their games with trick shots and fancy dribbling.

| 1987 | 1989 | 1991 | 1996 | 1997 | 1998 | 2007 | 2008 |

Patricia Summit was the winningest coach at any level of college basketball— male or female—when she retired from the University of Tennessee's Lady Vols in 2012 with eight national championships and 1,098 wins.

In 2001, the LA Sparks became the first team to win every home game in a season, ending with their first WNBA championship.

Lisa Leslie of the LA Sparks was the first WNBA player to be named MVP three different ways in the same season: for the regular season, for the All-Star game, and for the 2001 championship title.

ORDER ON THE COURT

For women, the court was originally divided into three sections, and players had to stay in assigned sections. Guards were posted at the door, making sure no men could watch.

The Women's National Basketball Association (WNBA) was announced on April 24, 1996, with eight teams proclaiming, **"WE GOT NEXT!"**

Since 1999, women's basketball has had its own Hall of Fame in Knoxville, Tennessee.

IN 1986, NANCY LIEBERMAN BECAME THE FIRST WOMAN TO JOIN A PROFESSIONAL MEN'S BASKETBALL LEAGUE WHEN SHE PLAYED ON THE SPRINGFIELD FLAME.

Women began playing college basketball less than a year after it was invented—and they wore long dresses!

JAZZ PLAYER

Lusia "Lucy" Harris was the first woman drafted by the NBA. She was signed to the New Orleans Jazz in 1977—but never played a game.

Over the Rainbow

Not only can there be double rainbows, but there can also be tertiary (three) and quaternary (four).

Hawaii is nicknamed the "Rainbow State" because of the frequency and beauty of the area's rainbows.

COLORFUL MELODIES

Two unique songs about rainbows made it into the American Film Institute's 100 Greatest American Movie Songs of All Time: "Over the Rainbow" from *The Wizard of Oz* and "Rainbow Connection" from *The Muppet Movie*.

Rainbows that occur at night are called moonbows, because they are caused by the light of the moon rather than the sun.

A Flag of PRIDE

Each color of the Rainbow Pride Flag has a different meaning: red represents life, orange is healing, yellow is for sunlight, green means nature, indigo stands for harmony, and violet represents spirit.

A Unique View

No two people see a rainbow the same way because of how the light is reflected through the raindrops on the horizon. Even your own two eyes see a rainbow differently!

ACCORDING TO NORSE MYTHOLOGY, A RAINBOW BRIDGE CALLED BIFROST CONNECTS MAN ON EARTH WITH ASGARD, THE LAND OF THE GODS IN THE SKY.

Word Search

Colorful Names

Look at the puzzle below and see if you can find the names of these colors. Circle the words going across, up and down, and diagonally. Some words may be backwards!

AQUAMARINE	GOLDENROD	MULBERRY
AZURE	HELIOTROPE	PERIWINKLE
CORAL	JADE	ROSEWOOD
CRIMSON	LILAC	SAFFRON
EGGSHELL	MAHOGANY	SAPPHIRE

```
D C K M V V M M E T U E P I E
Z O V L C Z A I N U P Y E W R
L R O Q J H Q F I O C Y K P I
F A D W O I Y R R E B L U M H
P L A G E E O T A H E C S D P
L G A Z A S O F M S G B Z B P
H N O I U I O N A F G A P U A
Y S L L L R O R U C S Z C S S
M O W E D S E N Q O H B F L Z
C H H G M E Q W A L E O O X L
P E R I W I N K L E L Q Z I N
P Z R D E N F R I N L J L C Y
N C U S A F F R O N I A A M O
H A B M V Q V R G D C K E B M
W B B C E D A J R U M G I E T
```

This and That

LOS ANGELES CITY LIMIT

The full name given to Los Angeles is **"El Pueblo de Nuestra Señora la Reina de los Ángeles de Porciúncula."**

Dreamt is the only English word that ends in "mt."

Maine is the only US state with a one-syllable name.

One of the most common pizza toppings in Brazil is green peas.

UNLUCKY NUMBER ONE

Daffodils are thought to bring happiness to those who receive them—but only in a bouquet. According to many legends, if you're given only a single daffodil, it can mean bad luck is on the way.

Some lipsticks contain fish scales.

Rubber bands last longer when refrigerated.

NO WORDS RHYME WITH "ORANGE" OR "PURPLE."

ON MANY PAIRS OF JEANS, THE TINY POCKET WITHIN A LARGER FRONT POCKET MIGHT SEEM USELESS, BUT IT WAS ORIGINALLY DESIGNED TO STORE ONE SPECIFIC ITEM—A POCKET WATCH!

Scotland's national animal is the unicorn.

Donuts sold in South Korea include the flavor "Garlic Glaze."

The majority of candy brands have been around for more than 50 years.

Almonds are a member of the peach family.

For Gamers Only

In the original *Super Mario Brothers*, Mario is able to jump more than five times his own height, meaning he's able to leap more than 25 feet in the air.

Sonic the...Doctor?

The SHH gene can be found in the human body and plays an important role in a variety of developments, including the front part of the brain and the eyes. "SHH" stands for "Sonic Hedgehog," named after the much-loved video game character.

In 1958, William Higinbotham created the first video game: Tennis for Two.

Nolan Bushnell helped create the Atari video game system and founded the Chuck E. Cheese chain of restaurant arcades in order to encourage kids to play the video games he developed.

A Creepy Mistake

The eerie-looking predator in *Minecraft* known as the Creeper was an accident. The game designer was trying to design a pig, but a mistake in the code created a stretched-out being—the now-infamous Creeper.

SEPTEMBER

Do you love playing video games? You can celebrate on **September 12, National Video Games Day.**

Space Gamers

In 1993, Russian cosmonauts blasted off for 196 days in space and packed a fun way to relax—a Nintendo Game Boy. Which game did the cosmonauts bring along to play? *Tetris*.

PIZZA INSPIRATION

The creator of *Pac-Man* got the idea from a pizza! Once, while eating the cheesy food, he took a slice from the pie and thought the remaining shape looked like a character. That pizza would become the iconic shape of Pac-Man.

RARE SPORTS

It's estimated that there are only around 20 remaining copies of *Stadium Events*, a 1987 sports game for Nintendo Entertainment System, making it a rare and expensive find. In 2010, a never-opened copy of the game sold for over $40,000.

CALL OF DUTY: MODERN WARFARE 2 IS ONE OF THE MOST EXPENSIVE VIDEO GAMES EVER PRODUCED, COSTING AROUND $250 MILLION TO MAKE.

RESEARCHERS HAVE DISCOVERED THAT PIGS ARE INTELLIGENT ENOUGH TO PLAY VIDEO GAMES.

Started from the Bottom

While working as a janitor and assembly-line employee at the Nintendo Factory, a Japanese man experimented with parts and made toys and electronic games. His inventions caught the eye of the company president who promoted him; he then went on to help develop early handheld game systems and, eventually, the now-iconic Game Boy.

Do You Believe in Magic?

Eye Tricked You

In the 1950s, not many people had heard of the magician's trick of sawing a person in half. When P.C. Sorcar performed this trick on TV and the television segment immediately ended, the station was bombarded with calls checking to see if the woman was okay. A news program aired later that night to confirmed that the woman was alive.

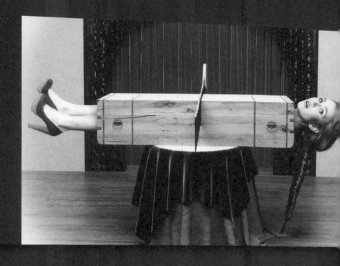

"The Man Who Fooled Houdini"

Dai Vernon, a magician and entertainer, certainly earned that title: Harry Houdini used to brag that he could figure out how any trick was done after seeing it only three times—but after Vernon performed his card trick seven times, Houdini still couldn't crack it!

The Library of Congress is home to Harry Houdini's personal collection of books on witchcraft, magic, and evil spirits—almost 4,000 books in total.

"HOCUS-POCUS," originally spelled "HOCAS-POCAS," can be traced back to the 1600s as a COMMON CHANT used by magicians and jugglers DURING THEIR TRICKS.

In 2016, the **Ehrlich Brothers**, a famous German magician duo, performed in front of the **largest recorded audience** for a magic performance— **38,503 people.**

PICK A CARD, ANY CARD

Close your eyes and picture a playing card. Did you pick the Ace of Hearts? Some researchers have found that when asked to visualize a card, people are more likely to think of that card than any other in the rest of the deck.

ACCORDING TO MEDIEVAL LEGEND, A SICK PERSON WOULD WEAR A TRIANGULAR NECKLACE ENGRAVED WITH THE WORD "ABRACADABRA," AND PEOPLE WOULD READ THE WORD ALOUD TO HELP THEM GET BETTER.

The Wand Chooses the Wizard

Head over to London to check out one of the world's oldest magic shops, which some say inspired the wizard's shop Flourish & Blotts in the Harry Potter books. Davenports, founded in 1898, is staffed by magicians who are eager to help any level of aspiring magician select materials, including the perfect wand!

Forget the Oscars or the Grammys: The Merlin Awards are given out to magicians worldwide for their contributions to the field of magic and performance.

BUNNY LAWS

It's illegal for people to keep rabbits as pets in Queensland, Australia. Luckily, magicians are one of the few exceptions to the rule.

HAT TRICK

Pulling a rabbit from a hat is a trick far more commonly associated with magicians than it is performed. It likely originated in the 1800s with John Henry Anderson, nicknamed "The Great Wizard of the North."

Destination: Wedding

AT THE END OF A TRADITIONAL WEDDING CEREMONY IN GERMANY, NEWLYWEDS MUST SAW A LOG IN HALF TO SYMBOLIZE THEIR STRENGTH AS A PAIR AND THEIR ABILITY TO OVERCOME CHALLENGES TOGETHER.

Pay It Forward

At Israeli weddings, guests don't bring gifts. Instead, they bring money—which the newlyweds will use to pay for the wedding itself.

BOTH FEET ON THE GROUND

In Ireland, a bride must keep her feet on the floor the entire time she is dancing. Otherwise, according to Irish folklore, she will be swept away by evil fairies.

GIVE 'EM THE SLIP

It's good luck for a newly married couple in Venezuela to sneak out of their own wedding reception without getting caught. It's also good fortune for any guests that realize the newlyweds are missing.

SHOES FIRST

Joota chupai is a fun Indian wedding ritual in which the bridesmaids and bride's sisters and other female relatives steal the groom's shoes. The groom's side must try to recover the shoes before the end of the ceremony, or the groom has to pay the bride's side to get them back!

Despite the time-honored tradition, it's illegal for wedding guests to throw rice at the bride and groom in Cádiz, Spain.

Show Me the Money

During the Greek money dance, the bride and groom dance while the guests come up to them and pin money on their clothes! Nigeria, Poland, and other countries and cultures have different versions of this dance.

A bride and groom in the Congo are not allowed to smile on their wedding day.

ABOUT **ONE MONTH** BEFORE THE WEDDING, TUJIA BRIDES IN PARTS OF CHINA CRY FOR ONE HOUR **EVERY DAY.**

Have Your Cake, and Drink It, Too?

In Norway, the customary wedding treat is a *kransekake*, a dessert made of layered almond cake rings with a bottle of champagne or wine in the hollow center.

PAKISTANI
WEDDING CEREMONIES
USUALLY LAST
THREE TO FIVE DAYS.

IN THE UNITED KINGDOM, A BACHELORETTE PARTY IS CALLED A "HEN DO" OR "HEN PARTY," AND A BACHELOR PARTY IS A "STAG DO" OR "STAG PARTY."

Creatures Great and Small

Really, Rhino?

The rhinoceros horn is not made of bone. It's made of the same material as hair and nails—keratin. However, rhinos still need calcium to keep their bones strong.

A swan can have over 25,000 feathers.

ELEPHANT VS. HUMAN

An elephant's trunk has around *40,000* muscles.

Compare that to humans, who have up to *850* muscles in their *entire bodies!*

IT'S THE TOOTH

When a horse bares its teeth, *count them* to tell if it's male or female: Males can have 40 or more permanent teeth, while females may have only 36.

Age Spots

How do you guess a giraffe's age? The darker the patches, the older it is.

CROC ON

The largest kinds of crocodiles live the longest. One giant freshwater croc, rescued in Queensland, Australia, by wildlife conservationist Steve Irwin, lived between **120** and **140 years.**

KNIGHTED KING

A king penguin at the Edinburgh Zoo is a real-live knight called Sir Nils Olav. The penguin—named after one Norwegian king and knighted by another—has been the official mascot of the king's guards since 1972.

A **SNAIL** CAN **SNOOZE** FOR **THREE YEARS,** MAKING FOR ONE **LONG** HIBERNATION!

FROGS DON'T DRINK **WATER;** THEY **ABSORB** IT THROUGH THEIR **SKIN!**

EAT UP, BESSIE!

Every cow has **FOUR STOMACHS!** The quadruple tummies help their digestion. Otherwise, they wouldn't be able to stomach all that grass.

ONE COW CAN PRODUCE **350,000** GLASSES OF MILK IN A **LIFETIME.**

What a Site!

The Not-So-Giving Tree

Feeling hungry? This tree is! The Hungry Tree in Dublin, Ireland, is about 80 years old and, as it grows, is slowly devouring a cast-iron bench.

If you can't make it to England's Stonehenge, take a trip to Alliance, Nebraska, to see **Carhenge**— a replica of the English landmark, made entirely of cars.

© Richard Van Der Woude | Dreamstime.com

IN THE MIDDLE OF THE **ATACAMA DESERT,** A 36-FOOT-TALL HAND CALLED *LA MANO DEL DESIERTO,* OR "THE HAND OF THE DESERT," GREETS TRAVELERS DRIVING ALONG CHILE'S ROUTE 5.

Topsy Turvy

Do you ever wonder how it would feel to experience the world upside down? The Haus steht Kopf, or Upside Down House, in Terfens, Austria, was built entirely upside down, with furniture attached to the ceiling, so tourists could get a new point of view.

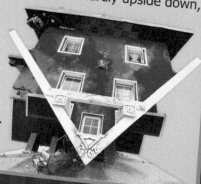

© Yorgy67 | Dreamstime.com

Icehotel is a hotel and art exhibition in Jukkasjärvi, Sweden, made out of (you guessed it!) **ice** and **snow**.

There are several **Cat Islands** in Japan, including Tashirojima and Aoshima, where **cats outnumber people.**

SEEING RED

The Red Beach in Panjin, China, is not a beach at all. Instead of sand, this wetland is covered in a type of seaweed that turns red from late summer to early autumn. The area is protected as a nature reserve, and only one area is accessible to tourists.

BIRD'S-EYE VIEW

Bukit Rhema, a prayer house for all faiths that draws tourists to Magelang, Indonesia, was built by Daniel Alamsjah in the 1990s after he received a holy vision. The building was meant to look like a dove to symbolize peace, but the locals thought it looked more like a chicken, earning it the name Gereja Ayam, or "Chicken Church."

The Big Pineapple, in Bathurst, South Africa, is the **tallest pineapple-shaped** building in the world: **56 feet.**

A Pyramid of Facts

Power to the Ladies

Unlike women in many other societies at the time, women in ancient Egypt were granted similar rights to men. They could own property or represent themselves in court, but only men were allowed to have high-ranking positions in business and government.

Wealthy ancient Egyptians owned a variety of exotic animals as pets: **baboons, antelope, lions, crocodiles,** and even **hippos.**

Because of erosion, the **Great Pyramid of Giza** has **shrunken by over 20 feet** throughout the centuries.

In the afterlife, Egyptians believed your heart would be weighed to determine if you lived a good life.

ANCIENT GAMERS

Senet was a very popular board game played by all. Wealthy Egyptians used fancy game boxes, while the lower classes drew the board on the floor.

Holy Beauty

Cosmetics were very popular with both men and women in ancient Egypt, as beauty was associated with godliness. Egyptians used perfume, foot cream, sunblock, and eye makeup in order to look their best.

The **Book of the Dead** was a collection of **spells** designed to help people's souls in the afterlife—no two copies were alike, as each copy was created specifically for the needs of the individual.

Crack the Code

Write Like an Egyptian

Ancient Egyptians used a form of writing called hieroglyphics, which was made up of pictures. Use the hieroglyphic alphabet key below to find out the answers to these jokes.

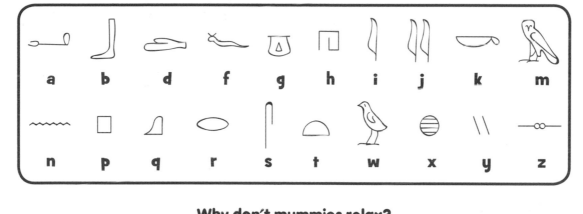

Why don't mummies relax?

_ _ E ' E _ _ _ _ _ _ _ _ O U _

What did the mummy say when he got a bad grade?

_ _ _ _ _ _ _ _ _ _ _ _ _ !

Why should you tell your secret to a mummy?

_ _ E _ _ E E _ _ _ U _ E _ _ _ _ _

Where do mummies go on vacation?

_ _ _ E _ _ E _ _ E _

Why are mummies bad gifts?

_ _ E ' E _ _ _ _ _ O U _

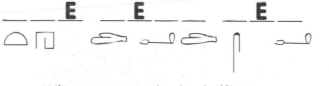

To Catch a Thief

CATCH HIM IF YOU CAN

One of the world's most famous imposters, Frank William Abagnale Jr., successfully impersonated a doctor, a lawyer, a law enforcement officer, and an airline pilot during his cons. After he was caught, Abagnale Jr. eventually consulted for the FBI!

In 2013, thieves in France stole just over **8,818 pounds** of **cheese**, worth more than **$43,000** on the black market.

Bejeweled Thievery

Doris Payne's 70 years as a jewel thief— using 32 different aliases— involved many memorable scams: In the 1970s, she stole a 10-carat diamond ring worth over half a million dollars.

DEAL OR NO DEAL

Notorious train and bank robber Butch Cassidy was so good at what he did that the Union Pacific Railroad once offered him a full pardon for his crimes, along with a job working for the railroad, as long as he would stop the robberies. Cassidy rejected the offer.

BOOK 'EM

An avid book collector, the "Book Bandit" took his interest to new heights when he turned to theft. He is thought to have stolen more than 23,000 rare or valuable books from universities and museums in around 45 states—the largest book theft in American history.

Moll Cutpurse, a thief in 1600s London, gained her nickname from her trademark method of theft— **cutting** people's change purses **directly** from their clothing.

Named after the movies, the **Pink Panthers** is an international network of **jewel thieves** thought to have committed around **380 robberies** between 1999 and 2015, amassing around 330 million euros, or about **$369 million**.

RETIREMENT PLAN

In one of the **largest burglaries in English legal history,** thieves robbed Hilton Garden Safe Deposit Limited on Easter weekend in 2015. **THE CATCH?** All of the thieves were longtime criminals between **60 and 78 years** old!

Dirty Job

In 1970s France, thieves infiltrated the Société Générale bank vaults to access their hidden gold, jewelry, and banknotes. How did the thieves get into the bank? They tunneled underground through the sewers.

Write On!

The **pound sign** or **number sign**, also commonly used as a **hashtag**, is officially called an **octothorpe**.

THE USUAL VOCAB

The most commonly used English word is "the." Other words that reach the top of the list include "are," "of," and "that."

The letter **V** is the only letter that is never silent in any language.

The **interrobang** was once a **punctuation mark** designed by an advertising executive to combine both a **question mark** and **exclamation point**:

The dot over a lowercase *i* or *j* has a name: **tittle**.

Now You Know Your AB…&s?

The ampersand (&) used to be taught to kids as the 27th letter of the alphabet in the 1800s. When singing the alphabet song, students would sing "X, Y, Z, and per se and." While it was eventually removed from the song, the final phrase morphed into the word we use for the punctuation mark today.

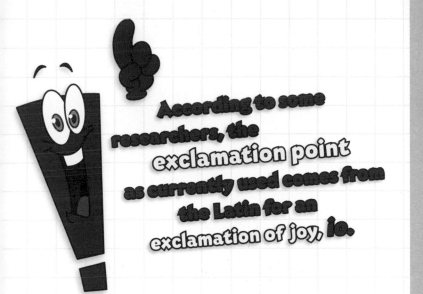

According to some researchers, the **exclamation point** as currently used comes from the Latin for an exclamation of joy, *io*.

A WORD CAN BE FORMED FROM **ANY VOWEL** SANDWICHED BETWEEN **TWO LETTER *P*'S:** PAP, PEP, PIP, POP, PUP.

French writer Hervé Bazin once suggested a variety of new punctuation marks, including the **irony mark** and the **love point**— which he thought could be used at the end of sentences like "Happy Anniversary."

SEEING DOUBLE

We pronounce *W* as "double-you" because of the way the letter developed. Old English scribes used to write "uu" for *W*, but with the invention of the printing press, writers switched to using "vv"—which then became *W*.

FREE OF ALL E'S

A lipogram is a piece of writing that specifically avoids using a particular letter or group of letters. For example, the 1939 novel *Gadsby*, by Ernest Vincent Wright, is famously known as the **"50,000 Word Novel Without the Letter *E*."**

TWO OF THE SHORTEST SENTENCES IN THE ENGLISH LANGUAGE ARE: "I AM" AND "GO."

On the Map

More people live in the state of California than in the entire country of Canada.

The shortest river in America is 201 feet long.

The First America

The only remaining copy of a 1507 map made by German scholar and cartographer Martin Waldseemüller was sold in 2003 for $10 million to the Library of Congress. It was the first map in world history to use the name "America."

PAPER TOWNS

A paper town is a fictional landmark added to a map by a cartographer, or mapmaker, to prevent plagiarism. If another map included that place, the original cartographer would know his or her map had been copied.

BECAUSE OF THE SHAPE OF THE EARTH, THE SPOT ON THE PLANET **CLOSEST** TO THE **MOON** IS **NOT** THE WORLD'S TALLEST MOUNTAIN, **MOUNT EVEREST**, BUT **MOUNT CHIMBORAZO** IN **ECUADOR** THAT EXTENDS **ALMOST 2 MILES CLOSER.**

EQUATOR

ECUADOR
Guayaquil
Tumbes
Talara
Paita
Chiclayo
Quito
Chimborazo
20,561
Cuenca
Marañ
Piura

Scientists recently calculated that the continents shift at about the same rate that fingernails grow.

AMONG THE PAINTINGS DRAWN ON THE WALLS OF CAVES IN LASCAUX, FRANCE, **A MAP OF THE STARS** WAS DISCOVERED THAT IS THOUGHT TO DATE BACK **16,500 YEARS.**

Due to shifts in the Earth's tectonic plates, the Himalayas **grow** an average of **2 centimeters** per year.

MOUNTAINTOP GOOGLING

Mount Mabu in Mozambique is known as the **"Google Forest"** because researchers discovered it while using **Google Earth** to find the right site for their research. They noticed geographic formations that were not labeled, and, upon traveling to the geographic coordinates, they **found forests** in pristine condition.

© Cosmin Constantin Sava | Dreamstime.com

CHINA

ALTHOUGH CHINA *SPANS ACROSS* FIVE DIFFERENT TIME ZONES, THE COUNTRY ONLY OFFICIALLY RECOGNIZES ONE.

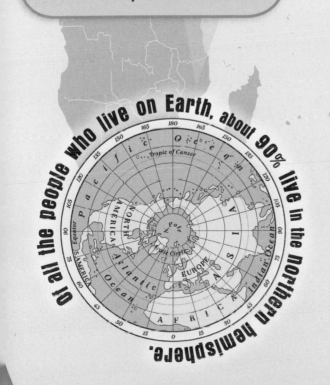

Of all the people who live on Earth, about 90% live in the northern hemisphere.

X Doesn't Mark the Spot

When researchers in 2012 traveled to Sandy Island near Australia, a place supposedly discovered in 1876 and included on numerous maps since, they found...nothing. The island doesn't exist!

The Most Important Meal of the Day

The average American spends only **12 minutes** eating breakfast, but **24 minutes** eating dinner.

12 Min

The restaurant chain **Waffle House** serves 145 **waffles** every minute.

Cereal Reader

In 1909, Kellogg's offered the first cereal box prize in its Corn Flakes® cereal. Customers who purchased two boxes could send proof back to the company in order to receive a book called *The Funny Jungleland Moving Pictures Book.*

DELICIOUS LOCATIONS

THESE REAL PLACES IN THE UNITED STATES HAVE SOME BREAKFAST-RELATED NAMES: TWO EGG, FLORIDA; HOT COFFEE, MISSISSIPPI; TOAST, NORTH CAROLINA; AND CEREAL, PENNSYLVANIA.

APOLLO 11, THE SPACE FLIGHT THAT LANDED THE FIRST PEOPLE ON THE MOON, CARRIED A BREAKFAST THAT REMINDED THE ASTRONAUTS OF HOME: **PACKAGES OF FROSTED CORNFLAKES** ALONG WITH **FREEZE-DRIED MILK.**

While Froot Loops come in many colors— red, green, orange, yellow, **purple**— they're all the **same** blend of **flavors**.

On average, an American eats **160 bowls** of cereal every year.

During World War II, the US government asked Americans to put their love of bacon to good use by sending the military their remaining bacon fat from cooking so it could be used to help create explosives.

Manchester, England, in 1994, was the site of the world-record-holding **largest pancake,** measuring over **49 feet wide**—almost as long as a **bowling lane.**

A MEAL FIT FOR A HUMAN

Ferdinand Schumacher faced an uphill battle in the 1850s when he opened the first German Hills American Oatmeal Factory: **Americans typically fed their livestock oats,** so they thought the now-popular breakfast food was for **animals!**

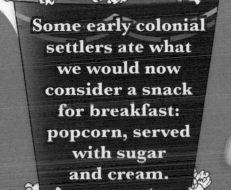

Some early colonial settlers ate what we would now consider a snack for breakfast: popcorn, served with sugar and cream.

Wish Upon a... Crepe?

Fête de la Chandeleur is a French holiday to flip for. One of the customs is to make a wish while flipping a crepe with one hand and holding a gold coin in the other!

Make Way for Villains

In the *Despicable Me* movies, the minions seem to speak gibberish, but it's really a mishmash of English, French, Italian, Spanish, and other languages, along with some nonsense noises—in other words, their own language: "Minionese."

C. Yudhistira | dreamstime.com

ACCORDING TO AUTHOR J.K ROWLING, PEOPLE HAVE LONG BEEN MISPRONOUNCING "VOLDEMORT"— THE "T" IS SILENT.

Snow White's stepmother is called the **Evil Queen** in Disney's 1937 film *Snow White and the Seven Dwarfs,* but her real name is **Queen Grimhilde.**

Walt Disney insisted on keeping Captain Hook alive at the end of the 1953 *Peter Pan* film, because he thought audiences would enjoy the character's bumbling, sneaky personality and wouldn't want him harmed.

THE ARMOR WORN BY ANCIENT JAPANESE SAMURAI WARRIORS STRONGLY INFLUENCED THE LOOK OF DARTH VADER'S SUIT.

FOOLISH FIENDS

While Batman often battles spooky, scary evildoers, some of them don't quite measure up to the rest. Take, for example, the Penny Plunderer, a man obsessed with stealing pennies, or the Condiment King, who uses ketchup and mustard as weapons.

JEDI MIND QUOTE

ONE OF THE MOST MISQUOTED LINES IN FILM COMES FROM AN ICONIC MOMENT IN THE *STAR WARS* SERIES.

MOST PEOPLE THINK DARTH VADER SAYS, "LUKE, I AM YOUR FATHER," BUT THE LINE SAID IS, "NO, I AM YOUR FATHER."

The word "orc"— best known as the name of the ogre-like creatures in J.R.R. Tolkien's The Lord of the Rings series— likely comes from the Latin *Orcus*. a god of the underworld.

Listen to the Music

MISTAKEN MELODY

A mondegreen is a phrase, often in song lyrics, **that is misheard.** Think of **Taylor Swift's chart-topping song "Blank Space,"** which caused a media frenzy when **many confused listeners** thought she sang the phrase **"Starbucks lovers."**

MOO-sical Tastes

Farmers and scientists alike discovered that cows can increase their milk production if they listen to music. However, like most humans, they have their own musical tastes: Slow songs in particular have a positive effect.

Songs to Shop To

Do you ever wonder about the music you hear in stores? The songs are specifically selected, as researchers have found that grocery store shoppers spend more money when slow tempo music is played, and flower store shoppers spend more when romantic music is played.

AQUATIC ANTHEMS

SCIENTISTS IN JAPAN REVEALED THAT SOME FISH RECOGNIZE SONGS AND CAN TELL THE DIFFERENCE BETWEEN COMPOSERS. WHEN PLAYED CLASSICAL MUSIC, THE GOLDFISH REACTED DIFFERENTLY TO PIECES BY BACH AND STRAVINSKY, SUGGESTING THEY COULD TELL THEM APART.

CHILLS, THEY'RE MULTIPLYING

Ever listen to a song and get the chills? It's more common than you think: Researchers estimate it happens to about 50% of people, and it's caused by the song stimulating a chemical pathway in the brain.

BEATS BY BALDWIN

In the early 1900s, Nathaniel Baldwin developed the first modern pair of headphones right at home in his kitchen. He sent a prototype to the US Navy, which adapted a version of the product to be used for radio communication on naval ships.

The world's longest musical performance—of a composition called "As SLow aS Possible"—started in 2001 at an old church in Germany and is set to conclude in the year 2640.

CAN'T GET YOU OUT OF MY HEAD

Don't you just hate getting a song stuck in your head? There's a word for those types of catchy songs: EARWORMS.

On average, an American spends over four hours a day listening to music.

Tasteful Traits

Research has shown that there's a connection between music preferences and personality types. For example, hip-hop is preferred by extroverts more than introverts, and those who enjoy jazz are often intellectual.

By the Numbers

Two and **five** are the only prime numbers that end in a **two** or **five**.

A Name Misspelled

The name "Google" was an accident. One of the site's founders suggested they name it "googol" after "googolplex" (one of the largest numbers), but another founder mistakenly spelled the name "Google."

A RUBIK'S CUBE, MIXED UP IN ANY CONFIGURATION, CAN BE SOLVED IN ONLY 26 MOVES.

OPPOSITE SIDES OF TRADITIONAL SIX-SIDED DICE ALWAYS ADD UP TO SEVEN.

Research has shown that people often associate numbers with gender—**even numbers** as **feminine**, **odd numbers** as **masculine**.

The **only number** with letters that appear in **alphabetical order** when spelled out is **"forty."**

Ditloid Activity

Count It Out

Ditloids are fun puzzles that use letters and numbers to represent a phrase. Fill in the blanks with the missing letters to finish the phrases. The first one has been completed for you.

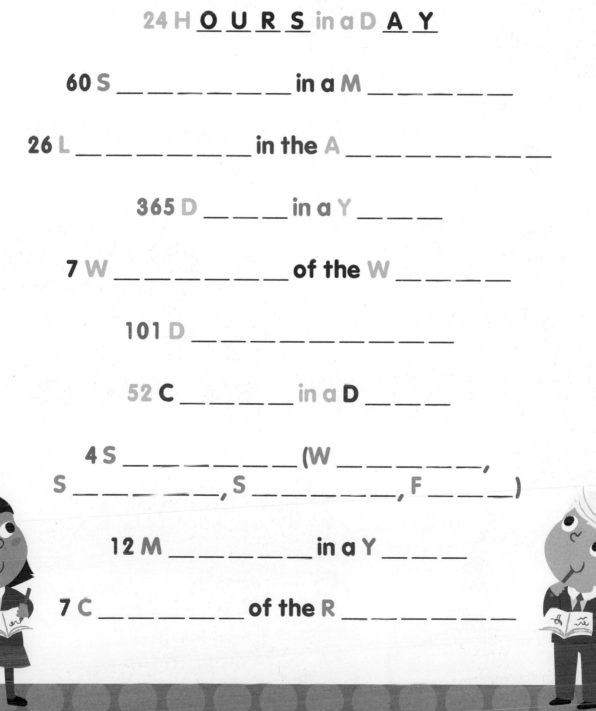

24 H **O U R S** in a D **A Y**

60 S _ _ _ _ _ _ _ in a M _ _ _ _ _ _

26 L _ _ _ _ _ _ _ in the A _ _ _ _ _ _ _ _

365 D _ _ _ in a Y _ _ _ _

7 W _ _ _ _ _ _ _ of the W _ _ _ _

101 D _ _ _ _ _ _ _ _ _ _

52 C _ _ _ _ _ in a D _ _ _ _

4 S _ _ _ _ _ _ _ (W _ _ _ _ _ ,
S _ _ _ _ _ _ , S _ _ _ _ _ _ , F _ _ _ _)

12 M _ _ _ _ _ _ in a Y _ _ _ _

7 C _ _ _ _ _ _ of the R _ _ _ _ _ _

Happy Birthday to One and All

A Familiar Tune

"Happy Birthday" as we know it has only been around since 1935. Likely adapted from a song written in 1893 by kindergarten teachers Patty and Mildred Hill called "Good Morning to All," the lyrics were later changed to the festive birthday wishes they are today.

SEPTEMBER IS THE MOST COMMON BIRTHDAY MONTH.

IT IS EXTREMELY UNLUCKY TO GIVE A CLOCK OR A WATCH AS A GIFT IN CHINA BECAUSE IT REPRESENTS TIME RUNNING OUT.

IN JAMAICA, FRIENDS AND FAMILY TRADITIONALLY THROW FLOUR AT SOMEONE ON THAT PERSON'S BIRTHDAY.

Make a Wish

Ancient Greeks were likely the first to associate candles with birthdays. Cakes were made as offerings to Artemis, goddess of the moon, and candles were added to give the gifts a lunar glow.

BIRTHDAY MATH

On any day of the year worldwide, over **17 million people** are **celebrating a birthday.** According to the "**Birthday Paradox,**" if you ask **23 different people** when their birthdays are, there is about a **50% chance** that **two of them share** the **same day.**

BABY'S FIRST FUTURE

First birthdays are quite special according to Korean tradition, and parents throw their babies a *dol* ceremony. The birthday baby is placed in front of a group of objects such as food, **money, books,** art, or **music supplies,** and the item the baby grabs is thought to **symbolize their future.**

Vietnam's biggest holiday is Tết, the first day of a new year, when everyone in the country celebrates their birthdays together.

YOUR GOLDEN BIRTHDAY, SOMETIMES CALLED YOUR LUCKY BIRTHDAY, HAPPENS ONLY ONCE— WHEN YOU TURN THE SAME AGE AS THE DATE YOU WERE BORN.

Fast Facts

Countries often have **unique items** on their McDonald's menus, such as the **Veg Pizza McPuff** in India, the **Samurai Pork Burger** in Thailand, and the **McPinto Deluxe** in Costa Rica.

Best Out of Five

Dave Thomas tried out each of his five children's names for his new restaurant before settling on the one he thought sounded best: Wendy. The fast-food chain is named after his daughter, and the girl in the logo is modeled after her, too.

McDonald's once counted some now-famous faces among its restaurant employees: Jeff Bezos, the founder of Amazon, and Lin-Manuel Miranda, the creator of the smash hit musical Hamilton.

Wendy's®
QUALITY IS OUR RECIPE
NOW OPEN
TRY OUR NEW BACON
MOZZARELLA BURGER

EVERY SECOND, **75** HAMBURGERS ARE SOLD BY McDONALD'S.

← Welcome →
24 hours DRIVE-THRU

In the United States, you are never more than **←145 miles→** from a McDonald's.

SPICY SECRETS

To this day, the original secret recipe of KFC's 11 herbs and spices is kept under lock and key. It's in a top secret safe in the company offices, and only a few people have ever read it.

In **Japan**, Burger King once released a cologne, **"Flame-Grilled Fragrance,"** that was supposed to **smell** just like the restaurant's Whopper burger.

Subway once faced a lawsuit that accused the sandwich makers of selling **11-inch sandwiches** instead of the **foot-long sandwiches** claimed in their advertisements.

THE FIRST TACOS AT TACO BELL ONLY COST 19 CENTS.

In 2012, Pizza Hut restaurants in the United Kingdom created quite a buzz with their limited edition creation: Hot Dog Stuffed Crust Pizza.

SPEEDY SERVICE

In-N-Out Burger was the first fast-food restaurant with two-way speakers for the drive-through. Before those, employees called carhops had to physically go out to each car to take an order.

ALMOST EVERY **IN-N-OUT BURGER** LOCATION HAS **TWO PALM TREES** THAT ARE BENT TO GROW ACROSS EACH OTHER AND **FORM AN X—** INTENTIONALLY **MARKING THE SPOT** AS ONE FILLED WITH **TREASURE.**

Get Out and Play

Early versions of hopscotch courts were **100 feet long**—about half as tall as the Leaning Tower of Pisa!

IN MINNESOTA, KIDS DON'T PLAY "DUCK, DUCK, GOOSE;" THEY PLAY "DUCK, DUCK, GRAY DUCK."

YOU'RE IT

The record for the largest game of tag is held by elementary and middle school students from Elkhart, Indiana. Their game had 2,202 players!

In many countries, the "it" player in a game of tag is thought to be carrying a yucky, pretend thing worth running away from, like the plague in Italy, fleas in Spain, or "lurgy fever" in Great Britain.

Throughout history, the game of tag has been called many other names, including: "touch," "tick," and "tig."

KIDS IN ANCIENT GREECE WERE THOUGHT TO HAVE PLAYED A GAME CALLED *APODIDRASKINDA*, PLAYED EXACTLY THE SAME WAY AS THE GAME OF HIDE-AND-SEEK IS PLAYED TODAY.

TIRE PARK, TOKYO, IS JUST WHAT IT SOUNDS LIKE—AN AWESOME **PLAYGROUND** MADE OF OVER 3,000 **TIRES** BUILT INTO **OBSTACLE COURSES** AND SHAPED INTO CREATURES LIKE **ROBOTS** AND **DINOSAURS**.

Championship Seekers

In Italy, adults compete in the international Hide-and-Seek Championship. In 2017, 80 teams from all over the world played the childhood game in an abandoned Italian town.

WHILE PICK-UP-STICKS TODAY ARE MADE OF WOOD OR PLASTIC, KIDS IN THE EARLY 1700s PLAYED WITH STICKS MADE OF IVORY OR BONE.

Jump on It

Dutch settlers who moved to the United States in the 1600s brought with them a popular pastime—**jumping rope.** At the time, the English settlers found the game to be ridiculous and started calling the version using two ropes **"Double Dutch"** as an insult. The name stuck!

Ain't No Acorn High Enough

Climbing trees takes on a whole new meaning at the Pod Playground in Australia. The play area contains huge treehouse-like structures shaped like acorns, complete with tunnels connecting them for kids to climb up and in between, and slide down.

249

This and That

The word "origami" comes from the Japanese *oru*, "to fold," and *kami*, meaning "paper."

Carrot Vision

During World War II, British Intelligence didn't want the Germans knowing about their radar advancements to spot enemy aircrafts, so they started a rumor that the enhanced detection was due to their soldiers eating lots of carrots. British citizens believed the rumor, which still persists today, and would eat carrots during raid blackouts to increase their vision!

DURING THE MIDDLE AGES, "ONE MOMENT" WAS A SPECIFIC MEASURE OF TIME: 90 SECONDS.

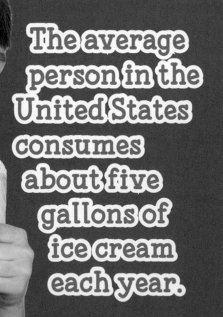

The average person in the United States consumes about five gallons of ice cream each year.

THERE ARE NO **STOP** SIGNS IN THE ENTIRE CITY OF PARIS.

GUN(TER) IT

Albert Gunter, local double-decker bus driver, was driving across the Tower Bridge in London when the bridge started to raise and separate to allow a ship to pass through. Gunter sped up and jumped the bus across the widening gap in the bridge—leaving passengers with only minor injuries and earning Gunter a £10 reward for bravery.

On the Left

Of the five US presidents that served from 1981 to 2016, four of them were left-handed (George W. Bush was the only right-handed one of the bunch). This is especially notable as there have only been eight left-handed presidents in all of history!

The Royal Canadian Mint once made the world's first coin worth **1 million** Canadian dollars.

Located off the coast of Dubai, the man-made Palm Islands are precisely what their name suggests—islands created in the shape of a palm tree.

When using a typical position on the keyboard, the left hand does 56% of the typing.

OAHU, HAWAII, IS HOME TO A UNIQUE NATURAL PHENOMENON CALLED THE UPSIDE DOWN WATERFALL, WHICH, AS THE NAME SUGGESTS, IS A WATERFALL THAT FLOWS IN AN UPWARD DIRECTION.

Greek-ing Out

Family Feud

According to myth, Athena, goddess of wisdom, and Poseidon each wanted a beautiful city to be named after themselves. Zeus asked them each to give a gift to the city's king, and whoever gave a better gift would win—thus, the city of Athens was born.

Godly Inspiration

NASA's 1960s missions to land humans on the moon were called the Apollo missions, after the god of poetry, music, archery, and the sun. According to myth, Apollo pulled the sun on its route across the sky every day.

Great Dionysia was an annual ancient Greek festival in which playwrights would perform their dramas in front of thousands of citizens in celebration of the festival's namesake Dionysus, god of theater.

Pick a Straw, Any Straw

When Hades and his brothers Zeus and Poseidon divided the kingdom amongst themselves, they did so "by lot"—which means they drew straws. Hades became king of the underworld, Zeus became god of the sky, and Poseidon ruled the sea.

Located in Turkey, the Temple of Artemis, goddess of the hunt, was a marvel for both its grand size and for all the spectacular works of art displayed inside, making it one of the Seven Wonders of the Ancient World.

Some ancient Greeks were thought to dedicate their sneezes to Demeter, goddess of agriculture.

The word "hypnosis" comes from Hypnos, the personification of sleep.

Crossword Puzzle
Greek Gods and Goddesses

Complete the crossword using the clues below. For help, look at the page of facts about gods and goddesses.

ACROSS

6. Goddess of the harvest and agriculture
8. God of theater and wine
9. God of music, art, medicine, sun, and knowledge
10. God of the sky

DOWN

1. Goddess of wild animals, the moon, the hunt, and vegetation
2. Goddess of victory
3. God of the sea
4. Goddess of wisdom, reason, and war
5. God of the underworld
7. God of sleep

Pencil in These Facts

The word "pencil" comes from the Latin *peniculus*, or "hair-pencil," as well as the French *pincel*, meaning "artist's paintbrush."

During World War II, British Secret Agent Charles Fraser Smith designed a secret map and compass hidden under the eraser of a pencil that was given out to British bombers in case they were captured in enemy territory.

A single pencil typically has enough graphite to write around 45,000 words.

The RECORD for the WORLD'S LARGEST PENCIL was achieved in 2007 with a pencil that weighed 21,700 POUNDS—about FOUR TIMES as HEAVY as a GIRAFFE!

Space Scribbles

Astronauts used pencils to write with in space, but they became safety hazards when the tips broke off and floated around the ships. Inventor Paul Fisher then developed the Space Pen, a pen with ink in a special cartridge that could be used without gravity. Fisher's pens have been used on spaceflights by both Americans and Russians since the 1960s.

JUN 10

National Ballpoint Pen Day is celebrated June 10 to mark the day brothers Laszlo and Gyorgy Biro filed the patent in 1943 for their brand-new invention.

Number the Pencils

Ever wonder what the "2" on your pencil means? The number on the pencil refers to the hardness of the lead inside: Higher numbers mean harder lead, which leads to lighter marks when writing.

According to some historians, pencil makers in the 1800s painted their pencils yellow to represent luxury because their materials came from China, where the color yellow is associated with royalty.

BEFORE ERASERS WERE INVENTED, PEOPLE WOULD USE BREADCRUMBS TO REMOVE PENCIL MARKS.

A typical ballpoint pen can do over 1 mile's worth of writing before running out of ink.

You're a Grand Old Flag

Passed by Congress in 1942, the US Flag Code details the guidelines for not only when to display the American flag, but how both buildings and citizens are required to hold it at a level of honor.

A FLAG DIVIDED

The two colored stripes on the national flag of the Philippines—red for patriotism, blue for peace and justice—correspond with the state of the country. The blue stripe is on top during peacetime, while the flag is flipped and the red stripe flies above during wartime.

The nine stripes of white on the Greek flag represent the nine syllables of the national phrase *Eleftheria i thanatos*, which means "freedom or death."

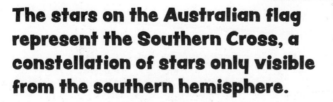

The stars on the Australian flag represent the Southern Cross, a constellation of stars only visible from the southern hemisphere.

The entire Norwegian flag can be divided up into segments that contain the designs of flags from six other countries: Poland, Thailand, France, Indonesia, Netherlands, and Finland.

The five colors that make up the rings on the Olympic flag were chosen because, in the early 1900s, when the flag was created, all countries participating in the Olympics had national flags represented by at least one of those five colors.

Switzerland and Vatican City are the only countries with SQUARE flags.

Hawaii is the only US state with a state flag that includes a Union Jack— a symbol of the United Kingdom.

Every Heart Beats True

The American flag is red, white, and blue—but what do those colors represent? White represents purity and innocence, red means hardness and valor, and blue is perseverance and justice.

Paled Patriotism

America planted a flag on the moon during the 1969 moon landing. Because of the moon's environment— days of either bright sunlight and heat, or freezing temperatures and total darkness—the flag's colors will likely be totally bleached and unrecognizable now.

What's in a Name?

With 26 first names (one for each letter of the alphabet) and a surname with almost 700 letters,

Hubert B.
WOLFESCHLEGELSTEINHAUSENBERGERDORFF

long held the record for the longest name— and that's the abbreviated version!

The first US Census in 1790 recorded the names of all US residents at the time, including some especially curious names: Hannah Cheese, Snow Frost, Mercy Pepper, and Agreen Crabtree.

Job Titles

Researchers have found that some jobs are more likely to be held by people with certain names. For example, firefighters are typically Ryans or Brandons, hairdressers are often Patricias or Loris, and veterinarians are commonly Tracys or Larrys.

In 2017, a group of 2,325 people gathered together to achieve the Guinness World Record for largest gathering of people with the same first name—Ivan.

What's-Her-Name

Nowadays, many people have surnames that originated in England. Historically, last names were created to describe various traits: occupations, personal characteristics, ancestry (the son of Richard would be Richardson), or places and geographic features (such as Lake, Brooks, Hill).

New Zealand's list of banned baby names primarily includes royal titles, such as King and Queen, but also includes a few symbols, like "." (pronounced "full stop").

THERE ARE LOTS OF SILLY NAME GAMES OUT THERE, SO WHY NOT TRY OUT A FEW!

ROYAL NAME

1. One of your grandparents' names
2. Your first pet's name
3. The street you grew up on

Lord/Lady _____ _____

of _____

DETECTIVE NAME

1. Favorite color
2. Favorite animal

_____ _____

SUPERHERO NAME

1. Second favorite color
2. Favorite drink

The _____ _____

JAMES

In the 100 years between 1917 and 2017, James was the most popular name for boys born in the United States—almost 4.8 million Jameses.

Middle names became popular in the Middle Ages when parents couldn't decide between giving their children the names of saints or names from within the family, so they gave each child both.

Given Names

The Icelandic Naming Committee keeps a list of approved names for all citizens—1,853 female and 1,712 male. Parents must pick one of those names or appeal to the committee to use a name not on the list, but, in order to preserve Icelandic culture and language, the committee approves less than half the requests they get each year.

Don't Try This at Home

SNAKE-Y LANDING

Known for his trademark red, white, and blue suit, famed motorcycle stuntman Evel Knievel's first jump in 1965 was over a 90-foot box filled with 50 rattlesnakes next to a pair of mountain lions. While he successfully made the jump, his landing broke the edge of the box and let out all the snakes, so the audience had to run away.

A HELICOPTER PILOT AND BASE JUMPER, FELIX BAUMGARTNER MADE A RECORD-SMASHING FREE PARACHUTE JUMP FROM SPACE IN 2012, BECOMING THE FIRST HUMAN BEING TO BREAK THE SOUND BARRIER.

Ladies First

The first person to go over Niagara Falls in a barrel was Annie Edson Taylor. To gain fame and fortune, she made the perilous journey in 1901 at age 63— and brought along her cat!

Although he successfully crossed Niagara Falls in a barrel in 1984, Karel Soucek didn't have the right permissions to do so and ended up with a fine of $500.

Walk the Walk

Jean Francois Gravelet, better known as Monsieur Charles Blondin, was an acrobat in the 1800s known for his tightrope walks over Niagara Falls. He made the journey on stilts, backward, with someone on his back, and holding a table and chairs that he placed in the middle of the tightrope to sit and have a snack. Not to be outdone, Maria Spelterini became the first woman to repeat Gravelet's stunts in 1876, crossing the Falls on tightrope, backwards, skipping, and with a paper bag over her head.

In a stunt nicknamed the "Tarzan swing," Steve Trotter sat on a small disk attached to a 176-foot cable in the center of the Golden Gate Bridge and swung back-and-forth, reaching speeds of 70 miles per hour.

The first man to climb all of Earth's 14 mountains over 26,000 feet, Reinhold Messner climbed Mount Everest without the use of supplemental oxygen—the first known person to do so.

Robbie Knievel followed in his famous father Evel's footsteps in 1999 when he made the death-defying jump his dad always hoped to achieve: over a part of the Grand Canyon.

THE FIRST PERSON TO COMPLETE LONG-DISTANCE SWIMS IN ALL OF THE EARTH'S OCEANS, LEWIS PUGH DOES ALL OF HIS SWIMS—INCLUDING THE ONES IN THE FREEZING TEMPERATURES OF THE ARCTIC—WEARING ONLY A SWIM CAP, GOGGLES, AND A SPEEDO SWIMSUIT.

Peaking Young

In 2010, at the age of 13, Jordan Romero became the youngest person to climb Mount Everest—and later the youngest person to complete the Seven Summits Challenge, in which a person climbs the highest mountains in each continent. (For the challenge, the geographic region of Oceania, which includes Australia, is counted as one continent.)

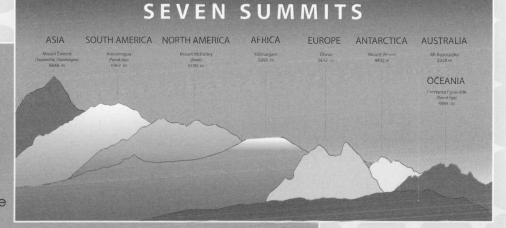

SEVEN SUMMITS

ASIA	SOUTH AMERICA	NORTH AMERICA	AFRICA	EUROPE	ANTARCTICA	AUSTRALIA
Mount Everest (Sagarmatha, Chomolungma) 8848 m	Aconcagua (Pinnacleral) 6962 m	Mount McKinley (Denali) 6190 m	Kilimanjaro 5895 m	Elbrus 5642 m	Mount Vinson 4892 m	Mt Kosciuszko 2228 m

OCEANIA
Carstensz Pyramide (Puncak Jaya) 4884 m

Fakes, Frauds, and Forgeries

Fakes are copies, replicas, or works that are mistakenly attributed to the wrong artist, while forgeries are works designed to deceive.

The cracks that form a network in a painting are called *craquelure*, and many experts use those details to prove a painting is authentic.

One of the Greats

Michelangelo dabbled in art forgery at the start of his career. After sculpting a piece known as *Sleeping Cupid*, the sculpture was placed underground so it would appear aged. It was sold, and when the fraud was discovered, the buyer was so impressed with Michelangelo that he became a patron of his original works.

Spell Check

A family in the United Kingdom spent years forging works of art by acclaimed artists, fooling places as esteemed as the Art Institute of Chicago. They were finally caught when officials at the British Museum realized an ancient sculpture the family submitted to them had misspellings.

A Display of Dupes

You can check out paintings that look like Picasso or Matisse at The Museum of Art Fakes in Vienna, Austria, but looks can be deceiving: The museum is filled with over 80 different famous works entirely created by art forgers.

Mistaken Identity

In 2018, the Étienne Terrus Museum in France, dedicated to the work of 19th-century painter Étienne Terrus, hired an art historian to help rehang the collection. Shockingly, the art historian discovered that about 60% of the museum's paintings were not painted by Terrus.

Spot the Difference

At the Museum

Find and circle 10 differences between these
two pictures of people at a museum.

I Want to Dance With Somebody

The rise of break dancing in US cities in the 1970s and 1980s led to the style being used as a way to settle disputes between local rivals who would "battle" for victory, which is why contemporary dance groups still battle each other.

While most people know how to dance THE MACARENA, many do not realize that the song of the same name is about a woman named MACARENA.

(Fort)nite Moves

Many of the numerous dance emotes in the video game *Fortnite* are directly influenced by movies like *Dumb and Dumber* and *Napoleon Dynamite*, as well as television shows like *Seinfeld*, *Scrubs*, *Arrested Development*, and *The Fresh Prince of Bel-Air*.

STEP AND REPEAT

In many classic Disney films, animators recycled animation from older films, especially for dance scenes. Scenes from *Sleeping Beauty* were reused in *Beauty and the Beast*, and moments from *Snow White and the Seven Dwarfs*, *The Aristocats*, and *Jungle Book* all appear in *Robin Hood*.

In Sweden, it is illegal for people to spontaneously dance in public.

Ride in Style

While "Gangnam Style" was the first YouTube video to reach 1 billion views, the well-known horse-rider dance moves took a long time to develop. The musician PSY tried various animals—monkeys, kangaroos, snakes, and elephants—before settling on the horse.

Put a Ring on It

Beyoncé's iconic "Single Ladies" dance was not entirely original. She and her choreography team took inspiration from a 1969 routine on *The Ed Sullivan Show* developed by Broadway choreographer Bob Fosse.

At the Ballet

The origins of ballet date back to Europe in the 1500s, but it wasn't until 1681 that women started performing professionally. Women's roles were previously danced by men.

In El Paso, Texas, over 40,000 people danced their way to the Guinness World Record for the largest group of people dancing the "YMCA."

It's Not Unusual

The famous "Carlton Dance" from *The Fresh Prince of Bel-Air* was dreamed up by the actor, Alfonso Ribeiro. The only direction given in the script was "Carlton dances," so Ribeiro combined moves from a Bruce Springsteen music video and an Eddie Murphy comedy special to create his character's iconic dance.

GOTTA DANCE!

In 1518, residents of a Roman city were struck by the plague...of dance. As many as 400 people supposedly felt an uncontrollable urge to dance that lasted for around two months. Despite how unlikely it may sound, it was thoroughly documented in historical records.

Crafty Facts

LOOK! SHINY!

Researchers have discovered a potential evolutionary explanation for why humans like glitter and metallic so much: It reminds us of the gloss of water, which our instincts know we need to survive.

Calligraphy

The word "calligraphy," which refers to the art of handwriting, comes from the Greek words *kallos*, meaning "beauty," and *graphein*, "to write."

SOME HISTORIANS BELIEVE THAT ONE EXPLANATION FOR THE PHRASE "THE WHOLE NINE YARDS," A TERM THAT HAS BEEN DIFFICULT TO TRACE, IS THAT IT REFERS TO THE LENGTH OF A BOLT OF CLOTH NEEDED TO MAKE A MAN'S SUIT.

Bitty Birds

A Japanese man makes some of the world's smallest origami paper cranes, using tiny squares of thin film measuring 1 square millimeter each. He had to create his own special tools to make the folds, as his hands and fingers were too large for the job.

THE FIRST SEWING NEEDLES, DATING BACK TO PREHISTORIC TIMES, WERE LIKELY MADE OF BONE, ANTLER, OR IVORY.

GLITTER BOMBS

Glitter was invented in 1934 by a machinist named Henry Ruschmann who found a way to grind down scrap pieces of plastic into the glitter we use today. Briefly, the US Army considered shooting glitter out of airplanes in order to confuse the radar of enemy planes during World War II.

SLIME TIME

Twelve-year-old slime-maker Maddie Rae held the first Guinness World Record in 2017 for making the world's largest slime—around 12,000 pounds. In 2018, her record was overpassed: The new amount to beat is 22,817 pounds.

GLUE

The United States experienced a shortage of Elmer's Glue in 2017 due to a surge in popularity of making slime, which counts the glue as a crucial ingredient.

THE **OLDEST HUMAN-MADE CERAMICS** WERE **DISCOVERED** IN SOUTHERN **CHINA** AND **DATE** BACK **20,000 YEARS.**

The FEAR of SLIME is called BLENNOPHOBIA.

EXER...CIT...V

IT'S A LONG STORY

Bayeux Tapestry, an important medieval artwork from 1066, is a detailed, embroidered tapestry that illustrates the Norman Conquest of England. It is 231 feet long— about three-fourths the size of the Statue of Liberty!

Reduce, Reuse, Recycle

In 1970, college student Gary Anderson designed the now-universal recycling logo for a contest to celebrate the first Earth Day on April 20.

THE **AVERAGE** PERSON **GENERATES** ALMOST **4½ POUNDS** OF WASTE EVERY SINGLE DAY.

On some beaches in Hawaii, scientists estimate that almost 15% of the sand is, in fact, grains of microplastic.

WHEN DEPOSITED IN A LANDFILL, IT TAKES A SINGLE HEAD OF LETTUCE 25 YEARS TO DECOMPOSE.

On average, one American uses about seven trees' worth of paper products every year.

Everything sold at the stores in ReTuna Återbruksgalleria mall in Sweden is either entirely recycled, reused, or sustainably produced.

Crayon-tastic Donations

Ever wonder what to do with all those tiny, leftover crayons? The Crayon Initiative is an organization that collects those pesky remainders from homes, schools, and restaurants and recycles them by melting down the leftovers to form new crayons, which are then donated to children's hospitals across the country.

According to the world's largest recycler of aluminum, if you recycle a can today it can be back on store shelves as a new can in as speedy as 60 days.

Flush Away

Scientists estimate that a typical person uses anywhere from 80 to 100 gallons of water each day. What daily action uses the most water? Flushing the toilet and, secondly, taking a shower or bath.

Scientists project that by 2050, the world's oceans will contain more plastic than fish. (Yikes!)

Gems and Metals and Minerals—Oh My!

You're My Only Hope

The Hope Diamond is a stunning blue diamond about the size of a walnut. According to some people, however, it's cursed. Those who have owned, stolen, or sold the rare gem have experienced failed marriages, insanity, bankruptcy, and death.

© Picturemakersllc / Dreamstime.com

Garnet gets its name from the Latin granatus, which means "grain" or "seed," because of similarities in appearance to pomegranate seeds.

GIRLS ONLY

The world's largest diamond, the Koh-i-Noor, is currently set in a crown displayed at the Tower of London. The Koh-i-Noor, which originated in India, is thought to be cursed—only women and God can wear the diamond "with impunity," or freedom from punishment.

Birthday Jewels

Birthstones have biblical origins, and scholars in the Middle Ages believed people should own all 12 birthstones and wear one each month. It wasn't until the 1700s that people began wearing the birthstone specific to their birthday month. The official birthstone list was created in 1912.

January		Garnet
February		Amethyst
March		Aquamarine
April		Diamond
May		Emerald
June		Pearl
July		Ruby
August		Peridot
September		Sapphire
October		Opal
November		Topaz
December		Turquoise

DIAMONDS ARE THE HARDEST NATURAL SUBSTANCE ON EARTH.

According to legend, peridot is thought to have mythical abilities to protect the wearer from nightmares and evil spirits and bring them into the light—so much so that the ancient Egyptians referred to it as the "gem of the sun."

The most expensive gemstone ever sold was the Pink Star diamond, a 59.6-carat oval, pink diamond sold in Hong Kong in 2017 for $71.2 million.

Cobalt is named for the German *kobold*, or "goblin," because of the dangers German miners once faced when melting down the metallic element.

Ancient Greeks and Romans often gave sailors gifts of aquamarine, a gem named from Latin words meaning "water of the seas," as they believed it would help sailors navigate safely through stormy seas.

FANCY FOSSILS

Amber is unlike many other gems because it forms from trees. The resin from certain types of trees drips down, trapping insects and seeds within it, and is then fossilized over many years.

While some minerals have pretty names to describe their looks, like fire opal or watermelon tourmaline, some minerals end up with silly sounding names, like goosecreekite, moolooite, and taconite.

Shipwrecked

Icy Remains

Last seen in 1915, the *Endurance* embarked on a Trans-Antarctic crossing but sunk after it was crushed by ice. The wreck has not been located, though some scientists believe it might be intact, frozen beneath a 5-foot layer of ice, 10,000 feet below the surface.

A Pirate's Life

The remains of infamous pirate Blackbeard's main vessel, *Queen Anne's Revenge*, were discovered in North Carolina in 1996. Scientists continue to recover artifacts from the ship, and their findings have included pewter plates, a spoon, the ship's signal bell, and cannons and cannon balls.

In a 17-mile stretch of ocean located off the coast of Fourni, Greece, 53 sunken ships have been located as of 2017, giving the area the nickname the "Shipwreck Capital of the World."

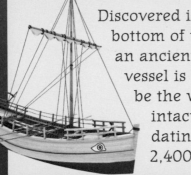

Discovered in 2018 at the bottom of the Black Sea, an ancient Greek trading vessel is thought to be the world's oldest intact shipwreck, dating back over 2,400 years.

Sunken Treasure

After colliding with another ship in 1905, the United Kingdom's *RMS Republic* sunk off the coast of Nantucket. The ship was nicknamed the "Millionaire's Ship" due to all its wealthy passengers, which led to rumors that it might have contained gold coins worth around $3 million at the time. That's more than $1 billion today!

According to Guinness World Records, the deepest shipwreck ever found was discovered in 1996 at the bottom of the South Atlantic Ocean at 18,904 feet deep—about the height of Mount Kilimanjaro.

What's Missing?
In Antarctica

Complete the scene by matching the pictures below with where they belong in the scene. Write the number of each picture in the correct blank. Not all of the pictures will be used.

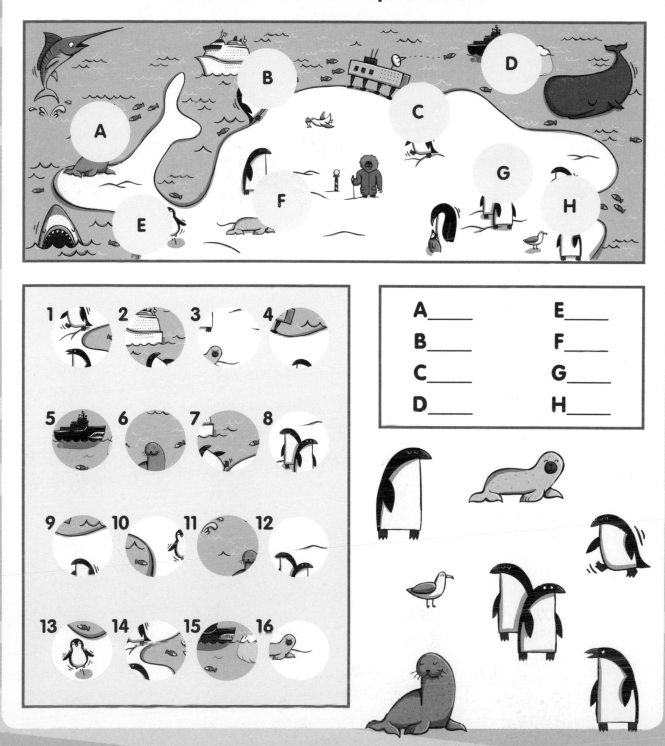

A_____   E_____
B_____   F_____
C_____   G_____
D_____   H_____

Spotlight on the Presidents

GEORGE WASHINGTON was the only president to get **EVERY SINGLE VOTE—** both times he ran!

Criminal Commute

James Madison and **Thomas Jefferson** were arrested in Vermont while taking a carriage ride on a Sunday. At the time, riding on Sunday was against state law.

It's All OK!

"OK," originally an abbreviation of "oll correct"—itself slang for "all correct"— gained popularity when President **Martin Van Buren** ran for reelection. Called "Old Kinderhook" for his hometown in New York, Van Buren's nickname was shortened to "OK" for campaign posters, and it spread across the nation.

Long Story Short

William Henry Harrison gave the longest inauguration speech on record—more than 90 minutes—but served the shortest term. In March 1841, Harrison delivered the speech while standing outside on a cold, rainy day and died of pneumonia about a month later.

Abraham Lincoln created the Secret Service hours before he was assassinated.

Tenth president John Tyler had **15 children**, the most of any president.

It's All Relative

There have been two sets of father-and-son presidents: **John** and **John Quincy Adams**, and **George H.W.** and **George W. Bush**. **William Henry Harrison** and his grandson **Benjamin Harrison** were both presidents, too.

One president was born on the Fourth of July—the 20th commander in chief, CALVIN COOLIDGE.

A BETTER LETTER

Harry Truman and **Ulysses Grant** both used the middle initial S. However, Truman had no middle name at all, and Grant's full name was Hiram Ulysses Grant.

WAR STORY

If **Lyndon B. Johnson** hadn't gotten off a military plane during World War II to use the bathroom, he would never have been the 36th president. The plane took off without him, crashed, and left no survivors.

The American President

Martin Van Buren was the first president to be a **US citizen**. The **previous seven** were all **British subjects**.

GERALD FORD PLAYED FOOTBALL IN COLLEGE AND TURNED DOWN OFFERS TO GO PRO FROM THE DETROIT LIONS AND THE GREEN BAY PACKERS.

JFK Goes to College

When **John F. Kennedy** was applying to college, his dad wrote a letter to Harvard University calling him "careless." He got in anyway.

Explain This!

The first recorded UFO sighting in the United States happened way back in 1639, when a local Massachusetts resident saw a strange, glowing apparition.

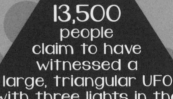

The Write Stuff

Archaeologists uncovered the Cascajal block, a stone slab with writing from the Olmecs, an ancient civilization in Mexico. The Cascajal block may be the earliest example of writing in the Americas, with symbols shaped like bugs, tools, and corn—but it has yet to be translated.

Around 13,500 people claim to have witnessed a large, triangular UFO with three lights in the skies above Belgium, but the Belgian Air Force has no logical explanation for what people saw.

Shine a Light

Since 1913, eerie and unexplained lights have been sighted near the Brown Mountain in North Carolina. While some researchers claimed that people were simply confusing lights from trains or other stationary lights, residents still reported seeing the glow even when a flood struck the area and knocked out the electricity.

Around the village of Carnac in Brittany, France, lies a stretch of over 3,000 huge standing stones in rows, called the Carnac stones, that date back to the prehistoric era—but why the ancient people put them there, and how, remains unclear.

Visitors flock to the Mystery Spot in Michigan to experience the small site—only about 300 feet in diameter—that causes puzzling physical sensations and optical illusions, such as making things appear shorter than they are.

Deep in the jungles of Brazil, British explorer Percy Harrison Fawcett embarked on many trips to locate an ancient indigenous city which, while never found, he referred to as the "Lost City of Z."

Name that Tune

In 1991, scientists from the US National Oceanic and Atmospheric Administration discovered spooky sounds in the Pacific Ocean. They named the odd phenomenon "Upsweep," but scientists to this day cannot identify the origin of the sound.

LOST AND CONFUSED

The "Lost Colony" of Roanoke was founded in 1587 with a group of about 115 English settlers, including John White, who sailed back to England soon after to gather supplies. Upon White's return, not only were the inhabitants of the colony nowhere to be found, but there was no trace that anyone had ever lived there.

RIDDLE ME THIS

The *Kryptos* sculpture, designed for the grounds of the Central Intelligence Agency, contains four sections of coded messages. Three sections have been decrypted, but the fourth remains one of the most famous unsolved codes in the world.

INVASION OF THE CLOTHES-SNATCHERS

In the summer of 1874, the Great Plains were attacked by trillions of Rocky Mountain locusts that ate not just crops, but also the clothes right off people's backs. While environmental conditions may have been a factor, no one is entirely sure why there were so many locusts.

When the Parade Passes By

Before the big procession takes place, Macy's Thanksgiving Day Parade in New York City holds BALLOONFEST, where each balloon is test-flown and the people who handle the balloons are trained on all the ins and outs.

Balloon Animals

In 1924, the first Macy's Thanksgiving Day Parade didn't have the gigantic balloons we are familiar with today: It had live animals. It wasn't until 1927 when the live animals were replaced with balloons, including a dragon, an elephant, and Felix the Cat.

Around 300 different marching bands apply to perform in the Macy's Thanksgiving Day Parade—but only 12 are accepted each year.

No Sights, Just Sounds

The Macy's Thanksgiving Day Parade was originally broadcast on the radio starting in 1932. Listeners of those early broadcasts had to rely on the announcer's descriptions of the balloons because they couldn't see the parade, which was first shown on TV in 1946.

Adjusted for Inflation

Flying a balloon in the Macy's Thanksgiving Day Parade is not cheap! It costs at least $190,000 for the construction and parade admission price, and an additional estimated $90,000 to get the balloon in that year's roster.

WILD WHEELS

Cruising down the street during the Houston Art Car Parade are vehicles of all shapes, sizes, and themes with new, wacky creations every year. Past parades have included a car with a large superhero figure on top, an ambulance decorated as a "Wolfbat," and a car entirely covered with plastic sea creatures.

© Anh Luu | Dreamstime.com

Hold Your Horses

The Federation of Mongolian Horse Racing Sport and Trainers organized the world's largest parade of horses in 2013—11,125 horses. The riders ranged in age from almost three years old to 90 years old.

THE **CARABAYA** PROVINCE IN **PERU** IS HOME TO MORE THAN **20,000 ALPACAS**, SO IT'S NOT SURPRISING THAT THEY HOLD THE RECORD FOR THE **WORLD'S LARGEST PARADE** OF **ALPACAS**—460—ALL OF WHICH WERE SELECTED BECAUSE THEY **QUALIFIED** AS "**FINE ALPACAS**."

Duck® brand duct tape was invented in Avon, Ohio, and is celebrated every year at the Duck Tape Festival, which consists of a parade with floats and costumes made entirely out of duct tape.

FISH OUT OF WATER

The Mermaid Parade of Coney Island, New York, is held annually during the summer. Participants dress up as mermaids and sea creatures, artists create intricate floats and costumes, and as many as 800,000 visitors have flocked to the spectacle.

© Fashionstock.com | Dreamstime.com

Call Me, Maybe

Extension POTUS

In 1877, President Rutherford B. Hayes installed the first ever phone in the White House, with a phone number that was simply "1." It wasn't until 1929 that Herbert Hoover installed a phone in the Oval Office, as all presidents before him used a phone in the hallway.

Don't forget to make a phone call on April 25—National Telephone Day!

Scientist Alexander Graham Bell, inventor of the telephone, thought that rather than saying "hello," people should say "ahoy" when they picked up the phone.

Ahoy!

Popularity Contest

Telephone **area codes** were first assigned in **1947,** with **86** set to represent the whole **country.** Numbers were **not** designated **geographically** but, instead, the areas with the **largest numbers** of **people** or the most **popular cities** were given the codes **easiest** to **remember** and dial.

Phone's for You!

Party lines, or shared, local telephone lines, were common in the 1930s and '40s, which meant that you could pick up the phone and hear someone else's entire conversation–and they could hear yours, too. You would know the phone was ringing for you based on the sound and pattern of the ring.

THE FIRST **911 CALL** IN THE **UNITED STATES** WAS MADE IN **1968** IN A SMALL **ALABAMA** TOWN CALLED **HALEYVILLE.**

LATEST MODEL

Released in **1983**, the Motorola DynaTAC was the **first cell phone** sold to **consumers**, though it's **not** quite like the ones we use today. It weighed **1.75 pounds**, took **10 hours** to charge for **30 minutes** worth of talking, and cost **$3,995.**

Petty Lines

Martin Cooper, inventor of the cell phone, made the world's first cell phone call in 1973, standing on a New York City sidewalk. Who did he call? The rival scientist who had been working on his own version of the cell phone.

The majority of modern cell phones in Japan are waterproof because of the popularity of bringing them into the shower.

According to research by the United Nations, more people worldwide have access to cell phones than toilets.

This and That

In Japanese, the word *subaru* represents the Pleiades cluster of six stars, which is what the car company Subaru is named after—and the inspiration behind the small badge of stars on their logo.

At one point, the US Mint considered making an official coin shaped like a doughnut.

Top of the Court

On the fifth floor of the US Supreme Court Building is the "Highest Court in the Land." No, it's not the Supreme Court—that's on the fourth floor. It's a basketball court!

MEDAL METALS

The Ages of Man form the general timeline in Greek mythology: The Golden Age, followed by the Silver Age, and then the Bronze Age. The medals for first, second, and third place at the real-life Olympic Games are given out in those same three metals in tribute.

The **Cadillac** car company originated in **Detroit**, Michigan, and was named after **Antoine de la Mothe Cadillac**, the French explorer who **founded** the **city** of Detroit in 1701.

Keep the Change

TSA collects and donates all the loose change left by passengers passing through security at airports. In 2016, that amounted to a whopping **$867,812.39.**

Contrary to popular depictions, in Greek mythology Atlas's punishment was not to hold up the Earth but to hold up the heavens.

The first Facebook logo in 2004 contained a face which many thought was that of company founder Mark Zuckerberg, but it was actually an image of actor Al Pacino.

Bubble gum is pink because it was the only dye the candy's inventor had on hand at the time.

MAINE IS THE CLOSEST STATE IN AMERICA TO AFRICA.

There isn't a single bridge across the Amazon river.

An Apple a Day

The rainbow apple is often considered the retro version of the Apple logo, but it is not the oldest version. The company's first logo from 1976 featured a detailed drawing of Sir Isaac Newton sitting under a tree with an apple about to fall on his head, along with a banner that read, "Newton - - - - 'A mind forever voyaging through strange seas of thought - - - Alone.'"

Written in the Stars

MONEY!
MONEY!
MONEY!

According to some superstitions, if you see a shooting star and say "money" three times before it disappears, you will come into wealth.

Looking at the estimated 6,000 stars visible to the human eye is like looking into the past, as the combination of the speed of light and the distance between Earth and the stars in the sky means that humans are only able to see stars as they once were.

To inspire kids to get out and search for constellations, The Big Bang Fair—a student scientist and engineering fair—worked with researchers at the University of Birmingham to discover and label eight new constellations based on modern figures such as Paddington Bear, Harry Potter's glasses, and Serena Williams's tennis racket.

The Big Dipper is often mistakenly referred to as a constellation, but it is, in fact, an asterism: a small grouping of stars that are part of a larger constellation.

OFFICIALLY, THERE ARE
88 CONSTELLATIONS
ASTRONOMERS HAVE LABELED IN THE NIGHT SKY.

Minnesota is nicknamed "The North Star State" because of the French motto that appears on the state's flag: *l'étoile du nord*, which means "the star of the north."

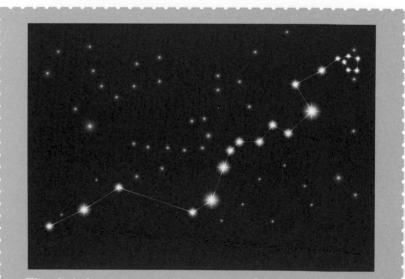

The sky's largest constellation is Hydra, which takes the form of a snake and covers around 3% of the night sky.

Connect the Dots
Constellations

Connect the dots starting from 1 to 7 to finish the Ursa Minor constellation, and from 1 to 9 to finish the Ursa Major constellation.

Ursa Major, meaning "great bear," is the largest northern constellation and includes the group of stars called the Big Dipper, in the bear's tail. The star in the tail of Ursa Minor, or "smaller bear," is Polaris—or the North Star—named because it has been in a fixed position in the sky of the northern hemisphere for centuries.

Connect the dots starting from 1 to 9 to finish the Taurus constellation.

One of the oldest recorded constellations is Taurus, the bull. According to Greek mythology, when Zeus fell in love with Princess Europa, he transformed into the bull Taurus to carry her away.

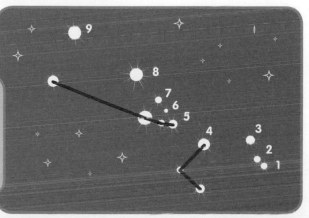

Home Entertainment

While there is only one Blockbuster Video left in the world, there are still video stores in the United States where customers can go and rent films, such as Casa Video in Arizona, Videodrome in Georgia, and Vulcan Video in Texas.

Competitive Viewing

Betamax became the first at-home video system in 1975, but a similar product, the VHS, was released only a year later. Even though Betamax played videos with better image and sound quality, VHS machines were less expensive and a VHS tape could hold three hours of video—likely an entire movie—which led VHS to entirely overtake Betamax as the dominant choice.

Home Movies

The **first film** ever released on **VHS** was a 1976 **Korean** drama called **The Young Teacher**. The first three **American** films released on VHS were **Patton**, **M*A*S*H**, and **The Sound of Music**—and **cost** almost **$70** each!

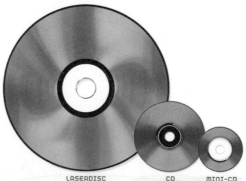

LASERDISC   CD   MINI-CD

TOO BIG TO CATCH ON

LaserDiscs, released in 1978, did not get as popular as VHS tapes or DVDs, likely due to two main issues: Each disc was about the size of a record, and each side of the disc could only hold about 30 minutes and had to be flipped over about halfway through a movie.

According to Reed Hastings, the founder of Netflix, he came up with the idea for the service after he checked out *Apollo 13* from Blockbuster and lost the tape—accruing a $40 fine.

Apollo 13

Of the 195 countries in the world, Netflix is available in over 190 of them.

NETFLIX

Netflix, founded in 1997, is older than Google, founded in 1998.

GLOBALLY, NETFLIX ACCOUNTS FOR 15% OF ALL INTERNET BANDWIDTH.

In order to provide customers with better recommendations, Netflix separates its movies and television shows into wildly specific categories, such as "absurd ghost-story comedies," "myth & legend children & family movies," and "exciting sports movies based on real life."

SILLY SYNOPSIS

In 2014, a programming bug hit Netflix, causing many of the one-sentence summaries of each movie and television show on the service to be combined. Wacky results included summaries like, "Legendary businessman and Apple co-founder Steve Jobs changed the way Americans live, think, and work before his extraterrestrial activity."

There's a Word for That

When you've got a word on the tip of your tongue that you can't quite remember, that's **LETHOLOGICA**.

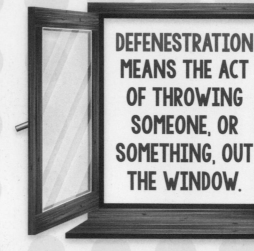

DEFENESTRATION MEANS THE ACT OF THROWING SOMEONE, OR SOMETHING, OUT THE WINDOW.

If you bring home ORTS from a restaurant, you are bringing home leftovers.

The earthy smell that happens after it rains is called **PETRICHOR**.

If you've ever pressed down on your eyelids when they're closed, you have seen **PHOSPHENE**—the impression of light when there isn't any light entering the eye.

Shake It Off

Have you ever sat in a position, like crossing your legs, for too long and experienced a tingly sensation often referred to as "pins and needles"? The medical term for that feeling is **PARESTHESIA**.

THERE'S NOTHING WORSE THAN AN ITCH ON YOUR BACK THAT YOU CAN'T QUITE SCRATCH; THAT UNREACHABLE PART OF YOUR BACK IS KNOWN AS THE **ACNESTIS**.

GRIFFONAGE is the word for hard-to-read handwriting.

CONTRONYMS are words with two opposite meanings, like how the word "left" can mean both "remaining" or "departed" (for example: "I left the party" vs. "I am the only one left at the party").

Usually made of cardboard, the holders that go around hot beverage cups are called **ZARFS**.

The **NURDLE** on your toothbrush is the amount of toothpaste you squeeze onto the bristles.

Bottled Language

Ever looked at a soda bottle and noticed it wasn't filled to the top? The space not filled in a container is called **ULLAGE**.

Getting up in the morning can be hard, and there's a word to describe that struggle: **DYSANIA**.

How I Spent My Summer Vacation

Among the Demigods

If you're a fan of Rick Riordan's Percy Jackson series, you will enjoy spending the summer at one of the many Camp Half-Bloods in places like Austin, Texas, or Brooklyn, New York. There you can become the demigod you are meant to be by strengthening your body with activities like sword-fighting or creating your own suit of armor, and strengthening your brain with Greek mythology trivia battles.

When attending camp at the Spy Museum in Washington, DC, your mission, if you choose to accept it, involves learning how to use a polygraph machine, analyzing forensic evidence, and even meeting a real-life spy.

In Indiana, you can go from a Padawan to a Jedi at **STAR WARS** Camp.

Prepare for THE APOCALYPSE at the ZOMBIE STEM CAMP in Massachusetts by learning about the science behind SURVIVAL: biology, math, physics, coding, and environmental conservation.

DO YOUR OWN STUNTS

Think you've got what it takes to be the next action-movie hero? Then head to the Pali Adventures Camp in California where you can develop all the intense physical agilities of a Hollywood stuntperson.

Bring your best jokes to the Gotham Comedy Club in New York City, which hosts a camp for aspiring stand-up and improv comedians.

One of the ways you'll train just like an astronaut at Space Camp in Alabama is sitting in the $\frac{1}{6}$ Gravity Chair which replicates the sensation of walking on the moon.

High school students can literally have an EXPLOSIVELY fun summer at Missouri University of Science and Technology's EXPLOSIVE Summer Camp, where students safely learn the mechanics of EXPLOSIONS.

◈ CIRCUS ◈

At the Future Stars Circus Arts Camp in New York, you can get ready to join the circus by learning the trapeze, stilt-walking, and, of course, how to be a clown.

YOUR KNOWLEDGE OF SHARKS WILL REACH NEW DEPTHS AT THE FIJI SHARK STUDIES CAMP, WHERE HIGH-SCHOOL STUDENTS GET TO DIVE IN WITH MANY DIFFERENT TYPES OF SHARKS IN THEIR NATURAL HABITAT: BULL, GRAY REEF, SILVERTIP, TAWNY NURSE, LEMON, AND TIGER SHARKS.

Spectacular Suites

Salty Accommodations

It took over 1 million 14-inch bricks to build the Palacio de Sal in Bolivia, but these are not just any bricks: They are entirely made of salt, as are many of the hotel's furnishings—making the Palacio de Sal the world's first salt hotel.

Tall Order

Travel guides often suggest eating where the locals do, and locals at the Safari Collection in Kenya include the giraffes that live on the hotel's sanctuary land. These elegant mammals often pop their heads through the dining room windows to join hotel guests for a snack.

Classic-car aficionados should speed over to Germany to check out the V8 Hotel, which has a variety of automotive-themed rooms—such as the Mercedes Suite, the Drive-In Cinema room, and the Car Wash room—all complete with bed frames made from cars.

VACANCY

If you're a dog lover, you might enjoy staying at the Dog Bark Park Inn in Idaho, a large building shaped exactly like a beagle with rooms full of books, statues, and art all about dogs.

BATMAN FANS CAN LIVE LIKE THE CAPED CRUSADER FOR A NIGHT AT THE BATCAVE HOTEL IN TAIWAN, WHERE THERE'S A SUITE MODELED AFTER THE BATCAVE—COMPLETE WITH ROCKLIKE WALLS AND, OF COURSE, A LARGE BAT SYMBOL.

Now Boarding

The Boeing 727 was a popular model of jet aircraft in the 1960s that could carry 130 people. In Costa Rica, one of these retired planes from 1965 was converted into a luxurious, entirely wood-paneled hotel nestled in the jungle canopy.

Designed in the shape of a volcano, with a waterfall trickling down from the top, is the Montaña Mágica Lodge in Chile, where the tiny windows of the wooden hotel rooms peek through the moss-covered sides of the peak.

PIPE DREAMS

Guests in Austria can cozy up for the night inside...sewer pipes? The owners repurposed old, large sewer pipes by dividing them into small, separate hotel bedrooms.

DEEP SLEEP

In Key Largo, Florida, you can stay overnight at a lodge located underwater. The only way to access the room is to scuba dive!

While backyard tree houses are common, a hotel in Sweden takes them to new heights with innovative designs, like a UFO, a bird's nest, and a cube built with mirrors to camouflage it among the trees.

Super Sleuths

Intrepid boy-detective character Encyclopedia Brown lives in Idaville, Florida, which is not a real place, although there are real Idavilles in Oregon, Pennsylvania, and Indiana.

Sir Arthur Conan Doyle wrote *A Study in Scarlet*, the book that introduced Sherlock Holmes to the world, in just three weeks.

All of the Nancy Drew books list the author as Carolyn Keene, but the name is a pseudonym for the many ghostwriters who worked on the series, including writer Mildred Wirt Benson who authored 23 of them.

Scooby Doo's full name is Scoobert Doo.

THE CASE OF THE MISTAKEN WORD ORIGIN

"Elementary, my dear Watson" has long been a signature phrase of Sherlock Holmes. However, author Sir Arthur Conan Doyle never wrote those words!

BAKER STREET W1

CITY OF WESTMINSTER

Puzzle Pals

There are numerous clubs and societies that honor Sherlock Holmes throughout the world. The mega-exclusive Baker Street Irregulars is rumored to require prospective members to complete a challenging crossword puzzle with facts about Holmes in order to join.

The character Sherlock Holmes has been featured in television and movies for over 100 years.

Mystery Words

Detect This!

Use your powers of deduction to figure out the answer to this mystery word puzzle. The answer is the title of a beloved, Newbery Medal-winning mystery novel for kids. Look at the clues to figure out the correct letter, and then write your answer in the box below.

1. The word for a baby cat has two of this mystery letter.

2. This mystery letter is the first letter of the shape that symbolizes Valentine's Day.

3. The word for the paper sleeve you use to mail a letter begins and ends with this mystery letter—and has the mystery letter in the middle, too!

4. The word for the opposite direction of east begins with this mystery letter.

5. Same mystery letter as the answer to clue number 3.

6. Two seasons of the year start with this mystery letter.

7. The opposite of "short" is the word that begins with this mystery letter.

8. This mystery letter is another way to say "me" that uses only one letter.

9. The first letter of the word that means the opposite of "yes" is this mystery letter.

10. The seventh letter of the alphabet is this mystery letter.

11. Another word for "smile" starts with this mystery letter, which is also the same as clue number 10.

12. Painters and sculptors are considered this profession, which starts with this mystery letter.

13. The first day of the week begins with this mystery letter.

14. This mystery letter is the first letter of the word that means the opposite of "begin."

$\overline{}\ \overline{}\ \overline{}\quad \overline{}\ \overline{}\ \overline{}\ \overline{}\ \overline{}\ \overline{}\ \overline{}\quad \overline{}\ \overline{}\ \overline{}\ \overline{}$
1 2 3   4 5 6 7 8 9 10   11 12 13 14

Winter, Spring, Summer, Fall

THE PHRASE "DOG DAYS OF SUMMER" REFERS TO SPECIFIC DATES—TYPICALLY IN JULY AND AUGUST—WHEN SIRIUS, THE BRIGHTEST VISIBLE STAR, RISES IN THE SKY AROUND THE SAME TIME AS THE SUN.

The feeling you get when the days start to get warmer, the sun stays out longer, and the world just seems brighter is often called "spring fever"—or, to use an old-fashioned word, "vernalagnia."

All snowflakes have six sides.

A Drink for All Seasons

Pumpkin spice has become a popular autumn coffee flavor, but it doesn't stop there: Many other foods are now available with that seasoning, including cereal, popcorn, granola bars, butter, chocolate, beer, yogurt, and even a hamburger!

THE **EIFFEL TOWER** **GROWS** ABOUT **6 INCHES** WHEN **EXPOSED** TO **DIRECT SUNLIGHT,** LIKE DURING THE **SUMMERTIME.**

Thousands of visitors make the trek to Stonehenge on the day of the summer solstice, the longest day of the year, when the sun is channeled directly into the center of the monument.

The word "solstice" comes from the Latin *sol*, meaning "sun," and *sistere*, or "to stand still."

Snowflakes are clear, but once the snow falls it appears white because of how the light bounces off the crystals and reflects all colors.

THE FEAR OF SNOW IS KNOWN AS CHIONOPHOBIA.

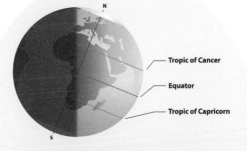

Tropic of Cancer

Equator

Tropic of Capricorn

During the summer solstice— the longest day of the year— the sun is at a 90-degree angle at the Tropic of Cancer at precisely noon, so nothing on the ground will cast a shadow at that time.

The Fall of Autumn

In 1300s England, the popular word for the season between summer and winter was "autumn," which replaced the more agricultural word "harvest." In the 1600s, however, the popularity of the phrase "the fall of the leaves" was shortened to "fall"— a term that especially took off in America.

BALANCING ACT

It's often said that on the vernal (spring) and autumnal equinoxes, you can balance an egg on its end because of some magical properties that only occur at those times—but that's false! It is possible any day of the year, as long as you know what you're doing.

Answers

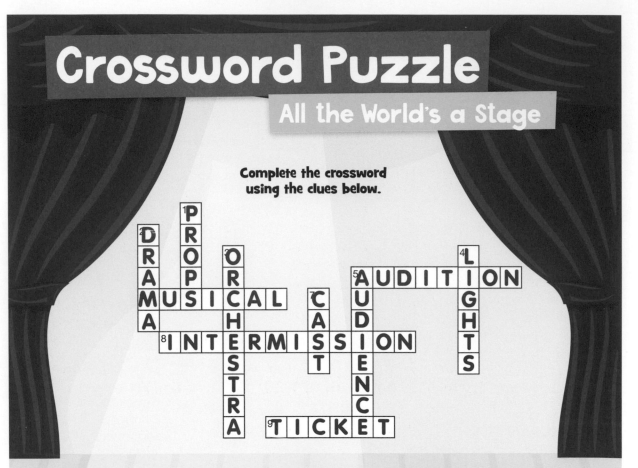

Crossword Puzzle
All the World's a Stage

Complete the crossword using the clues below.

Crossword answers:
- 1 DOWN: PROP
- 2 DOWN: ORCHESTRA
- 3: DRAMA
- MUSICAL
- AUDITION (5 ACROSS)
- LIGHTS (4 DOWN)
- CAST (7)
- AUDIENCE
- INTERMISSION (8)
- TICKET (9)

ACROSS

5. To try out for a part

6. A play with song and dance routines

8. The break between acts

9. You need this to see a show at the theater

DOWN

1. Furniture, pictures, or anything used onstage to create a setting

2. A serious play, without music

3. Musicians play in the _____

4. It's called the Great White Way because of all the bright _____

5. People who watch the show

7. All the actors in a play

Answers

Crack the Code
The Human Body

Use the key below to find out the answers to these human body riddles.

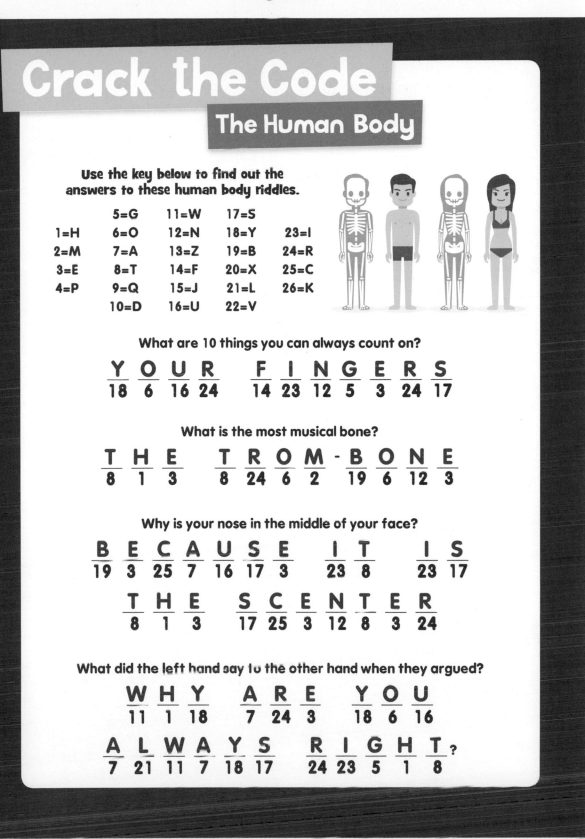

5=G	11=W	17=S
1=H	6=O	12=N	23=I
2=M	7=A	13=Z	18=Y	24=R
3=E	8=T	14=F	19=B
4=P	9=Q	15=J	20=X	25=C
	10=D	16=U	21=L	26=K
		22=V

What are 10 things you can always count on?

Y O U R   F I N G E R S
18 6 16 24   14 23 12 5 3 24 17

What is the most musical bone?

T H E   T R O M - B O N E
8 1 3   8 24 6 2   19 6 12 3

Why is your nose in the middle of your face?

B E C A U S E   I T   I S
19 3 25 7 16 17 3   23 8   23 17

T H E   S C E N T E R
8 1 3   17 25 3 12 8 3 24

What did the left hand say to the other hand when they argued?

W H Y   A R E   Y O U
11 1 18 7 24 3   18 6 16

A L W A Y S   R I G H T ?
7 21 11 7 18 17   24 23 5 1 8

Page 45

Royal Maze

Have Crown, Will Travel

Follow the maze from start to finish to help the queen go from Buckingham Palace in London to her country estate Windsor Castle.

FINISH

START

Answers

Word Scramble

At the Games

Unscramble the letters to spell the Olympic events.
Which event would you like to try?

EEPSD TINGSKA
S P E E D   S K A T I N G

OLEP LATUV
P O L E   V A U L T

NASTYGMISC
G Y M N A S T I C S

CHABE BOLYLELVAL
B E A C H   V O L L E Y B A L L

EPIPLAHF OWNSDROAB
H A L F P I P E   S N O W B O A R D

THALONRTI
T R I A T H L O N

TREWA LOOP
W A T E R   P O L O

Answers

Page 81

Crack the Code
Phobias

Don't be afraid to figure out this puzzle! Use the key at right to find out the official term for each fear.

1=H	5=G	9=Q	13=Z	17=S	21=L	25=C
2=M	6=O	10=D	14=F	18=Y	22=V	26=K
3=E	7=A	11=W	15=J	19=B	23=I	
4=P	8=T	12=N	16=U	20=X	24=R	

Astraphobia: fear of

T H U N D E R   A N D
8 1 16 12 10 3 24   7 12 10

L I G H T N I N G
21 23 5 1 8 12 23 12 5

Odontophobia: fear of going to the D E N T I S T
10 3 12 8 23 17 8

Xanthophobia: fear of the C O L O R
25 6 21 6 24

Y E L L O W
18 3 21 21 6 11

Coulrophobia: fear of C L O W N S
25 21 6 11 12 17

Turophobia: fear of C H E E S E
25 1 3 3 17 3

Phobophobia: fear of having a

P H O B I A
4 1 6 19 23 7

302

Answers

Fill in the Blanks

Every Letter Counts

There is a special kind of sentence that contains all **26** letters of the alphabet.

Fill in the missing letters below to complete the all-alphabet sentences. (Hint: If you're having trouble, look for letters that haven't been used.) Then write the numbered letters in order at the bottom of the page to find out what this type of sentence is called.

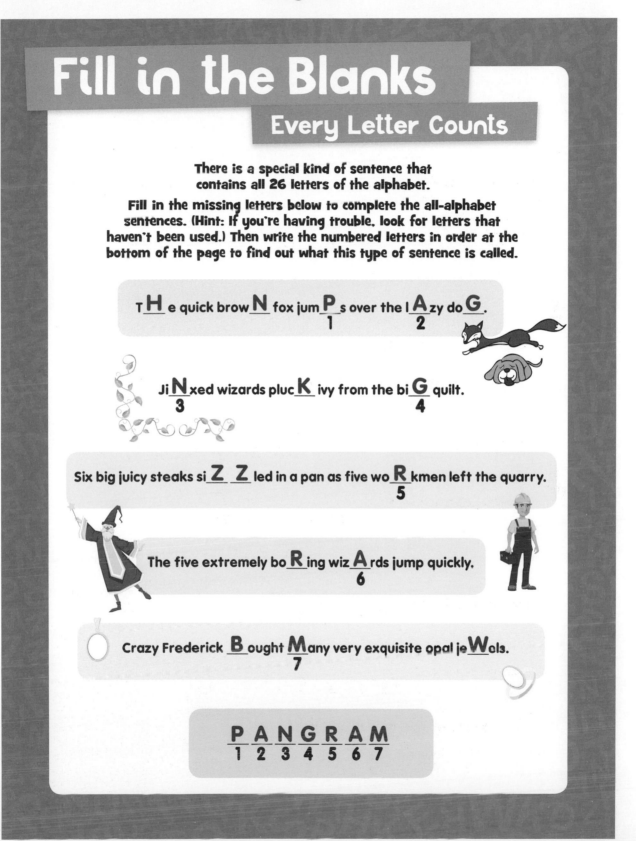

T**H**e quick brow**N** fox jum**P**s over the l**A**zy do**G**.
1   2

Ji**N**xed wizards pluc**K** ivy from the bi**G** quilt.
3   4

Six big juicy steaks si**Z Z**led in a pan as five wo**R**kmen left the quarry.
5

The five extremely bo**R**ing wiz**A**rds jump quickly.
6

Crazy Frederick **B**ought **M**any very exquisite opal je**W**els.
7

P A N G R A M
1 2 3 4 5 6 7

303

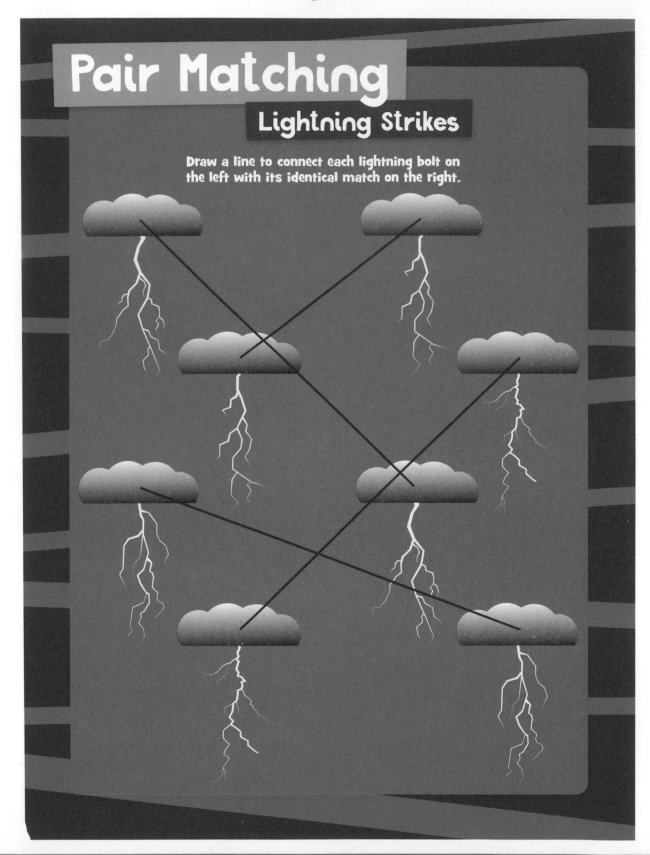

Answers

Pages 120-121

Answers

Answers

Word Search
Amusement Park Rides

Look at the puzzle below and see if you can find these names of amusement park rides. Circle the words going across, up and down, and diagonally. Some words may be backwards!

BUMPER CARS   **HAUNTED HOUSE**   **SLIDE**
CAROUSEL   **LOG FLUME**   **SWING RIDE**
FERRIS WHEEL   **PIRATE SHIP**   **TEACUPS**
FUN HOUSE   **ROLLER COASTER**   **TILT-A-WHIRL**
GO-KARTS   **SCRAMBLER**   **ZIPPER**

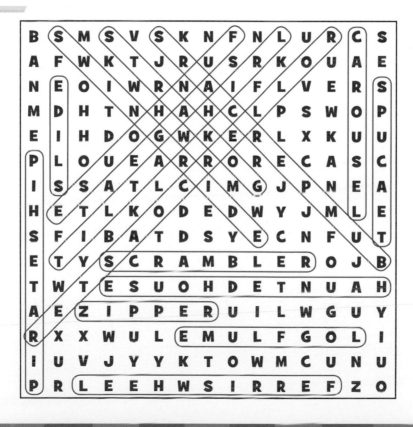

B S M S V S K N F N L U R C S
A F W K T J R U S R K O U A E
N E O I W R N A I F L V E R S
M D H T N H A H C L P S W O P
E I H D O G W K E R L X K U U
P L O U E A R R O R E C A S C
I S S A T L C I M G J P N E A
H E T L K O D E D W Y J M L E
S F I B A T D S Y E C N F U T
E T Y S C R A M B L E R O J B
T W T E S U O H D E T N U A H
A E Z I P P E R U I L W G U Y
R X X W U L E M U L F G O L I
I U V J Y Y K T O W M C U N U
P R L E E H W S I R R E F Z O

307

Page 187

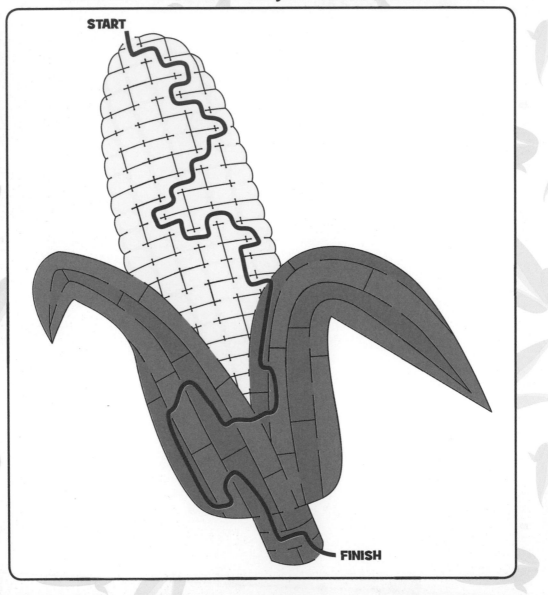

Maize Maze
Lending an Ear

One of the largest corn mazes can be found at Cool Patch Pumpkins in Dixon, California. It's easy to get lost in the maze's 60 acres of corn.

Follow the maze to see if you can navigate up, down, and around the kernels in the ear of corn below to get from one end to the other!

START

FINISH

Answers

Spot the Difference

Toy House

Find and circle 10 differences between these two pictures of a LEGO® house.

Answers

Word Search
Colorful Names

Look at the puzzle below and see if you can find the names of these colors. Circle the words going across, up and down, and diagonally. Some words may be backwards!

AQUAMARINE   GOLDENROD   MULBERRY
AZURE   HELIOTROPE   PERIWINKLE
CORAL   JADE   ROSEWOOD
CRIMSON   LILAC   SAFFRON
EGGSHELL   MAHOGANY   SAPPHIRE

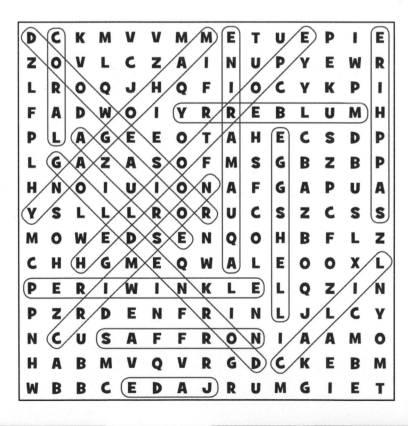

Answers

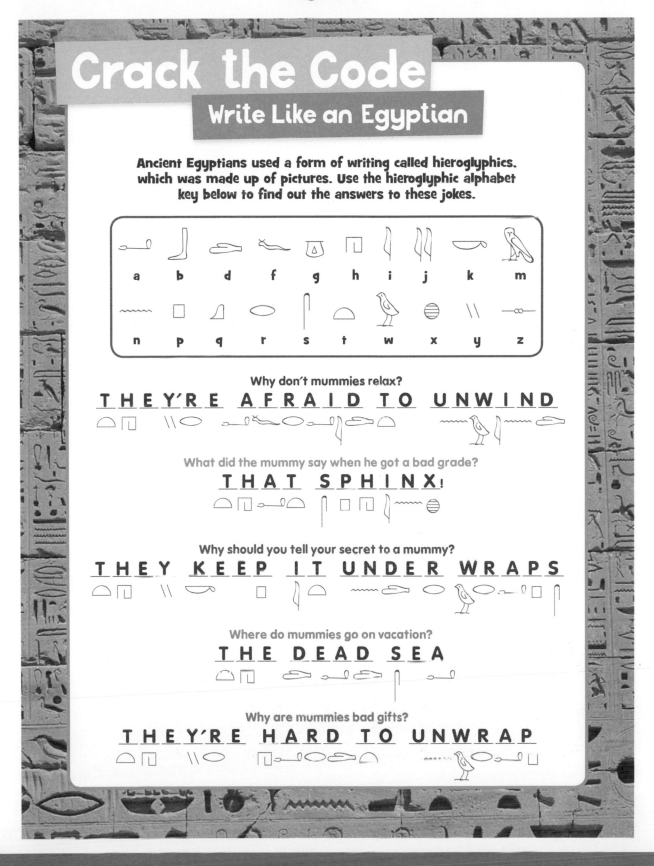

Crack the Code
Write Like an Egyptian

Ancient Egyptians used a form of writing called hieroglyphics, which was made up of pictures. Use the hieroglyphic alphabet key below to find out the answers to these jokes.

a	b	d	f	g	h	i	j	k	m
n	p	q	r	s	t	w	x	y	z

Why don't mummies relax?

THEY'RE AFRAID TO UNWIND

What did the mummy say when he got a bad grade?

THAT SPHINX!

Why should you tell your secret to a mummy?

THEY KEEP IT UNDER WRAPS

Where do mummies go on vacation?

THE DEAD SEA

Why are mummies bad gifts?

THEY'RE HARD TO UNWRAP

Ditloid Activity

Count It Out

Ditloids are fun puzzles that use letters and numbers to represent a phrase. Fill in the blanks with the missing letters to finish the phrases. The first one has been completed for you.

24 H **O U R S** in a D **A Y**

60 S **E C O N D S** in a M **I N U T E**

26 L **E T T E R S** in the A **L P H A B E T**

365 D **A Y S** in a Y **E A R**

7 W **O N D E R S** of the W **O R L D**

101 D **A L M A T I A N S**

52 C **A R D S** in a D **E C K**

4 S **E A S O N S** (W **I N T E R**, S **P R I N G**, S **U M M E R**, F **A L L**)

12 M **O N T H S** in a Y **E A R**

7 C **O L O R S** of the R **A I N B O W**

Answers

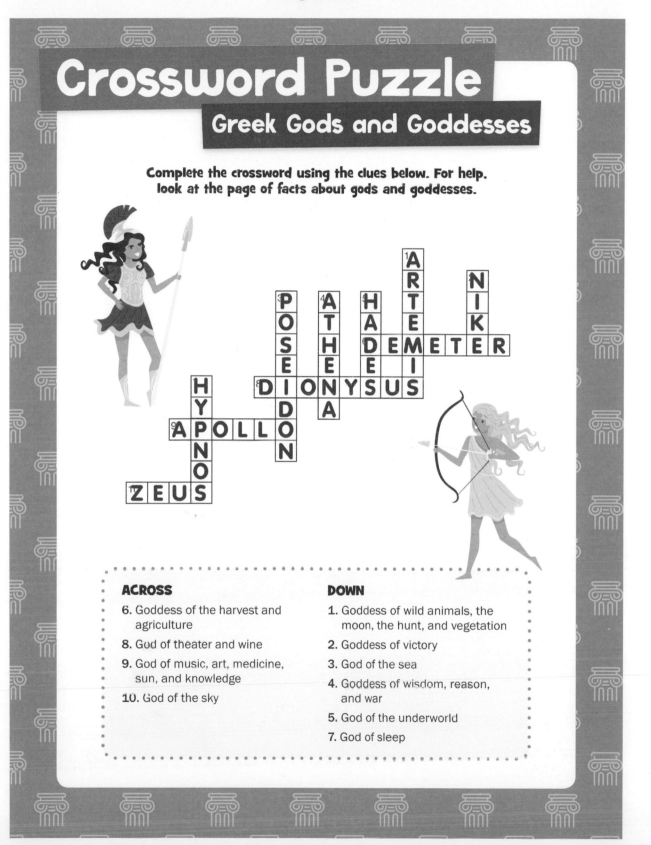

Crossword Puzzle
Greek Gods and Goddesses

Complete the crossword using the clues below. For help, look at the page of facts about gods and goddesses.

ACROSS

6. Goddess of the harvest and agriculture
8. God of theater and wine
9. God of music, art, medicine, sun, and knowledge
10. God of the sky

DOWN

1. Goddess of wild animals, the moon, the hunt, and vegetation
2. Goddess of victory
3. God of the sea
4. Goddess of wisdom, reason, and war
5. God of the underworld
7. God of sleep

Answers

Spot the Difference
At the Museum

Find and circle 10 differences between these two pictures of people at a museum.

Answers

What's Missing?
In Antarctica

Complete the scene by matching the pictures below with where they belong in the scene. Write the number of each picture in the correct blank. Not all of the pictures will be used.

A 6	E 10
B 7	F 3
C 9	G 12
D 15	H 1

Answers

Page 285

Connect the Dots
Constellations

Connect the dots starting from 1 to 7 to finish the Ursa Minor constellation, and from 1 to 9 to finish the Ursa Major constellation.

Ursa Major, meaning "great bear," is the largest northern constellation and includes the group of stars called the Big Dipper, in the bear's tail. The star in the tail of Ursa Minor, or "smaller bear," is Polaris—or the North Star—named because it has been in a fixed position in the sky of the northern hemisphere for centuries.

Connect the dots starting from 1 to 9 to finish the Taurus constellation.

One of the oldest recorded constellations is Taurus, the bull. According to Greek mythology, when Zeus fell in love with Princess Europa, he transformed into the bull Taurus to carry her away.

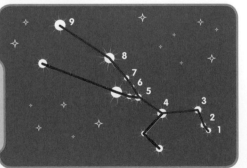

316

Answers

Mystery Words

Detect This!

Use your powers of deduction to figure out the answer to this mystery word puzzle. The answer is the title of a beloved, Newbery Medal-winning mystery novel for kids. Look at the clues to figure out the correct letter, and then write your answer in the box below.

1. The word for a baby cat has two of this mystery letter.

2. This mystery letter is the first letter of the shape that symbolizes Valentine's Day.

3. The word for the paper sleeve you use to mail a letter begins and ends with this mystery letter— and has the mystery letter in the middle, too!

4. The word for the opposite direction of east begins with this mystery letter.

5. Same mystery letter as the answer to clue number 3.

6. Two seasons of the year start with this mystery letter.

7. The opposite of "short" is the word that begins with this mystery letter.

8. This mystery letter is another way to say "me" that uses only one letter.

9. The first letter of the word that means the opposite of "yes" is this mystery letter.

10. The seventh letter of the alphabet is this mystery letter.

11. Another word for "smile" starts with this mystery letter, which is also the same as clue number 10.

12. Painters and sculptors are considered this profession, which starts with this mystery letter.

13. The first day of the week begins with this mystery letter.

14. This mystery letter is the first letter of the word that means the opposite of "begin."

$$\underline{T}\ \underline{H}\ \underline{E}\quad \underline{W}\ \underline{E}\ \underline{S}\ \underline{T}\ \underline{I}\ \underline{N}\ \underline{G}\quad \underline{G}\ \underline{A}\ \underline{M}\ \underline{E}$$

1 2 3   4 5 6 7 8 9 10   11 12 13 14